Welcome to Freedom Point

Welcome to Freedom Point

stories by

Marina Mularz

newamericanpress

Milwaukee, Wis.

n e w a m e r i c a n p r e s s

Printed in the United States of America

ISBN 978-194156116-4

Interior design by Rob Carroll

Cover design by Anneabel Gemmel
https://www.anneabelgemmel.com/

For ordering information, please contact:
Ingram Book Group
One Ingram Blvd.
La Vergne, TN 37086
Phone: (800) 937-8000
Fax: (800) 876-0186
https://www.ingramcontent.com
orders@ingrambook.com

For event and media requests, please contact:
New American Press
www.newamericanpress.com
newamericanpress@gmail.com

"The Wilderness" appeared previously in *The James Franco Review*.

For Greg Mularz
(1978-2015)
who spent his life rooting for small towns and little sisters

CONTENTS

Welcome to Freedom Point

CHEWING GUM WAS THE ENEMY. SO WERE LONG FINGERNAILS AND metallic gel pens. Cigarettes, real or imaginary. Curse words and baseball caps and glass bottles at lunch. For a short while, comic books with sexy drawings, too, but if anything was *really* destroying Freedom Point Junior High, it was the school-wide yawning epidemic.

Little local help was available. *Nothing* ever happened in or to Freedom Point, let alone medical miracles. Even most maps forgot the tiny Wisconsinian dot way-way up near the border, up where the state was barely still the state, up where life was allowed to nod off, for anyone, of any age. That's why Del Calhoun came to town.

IT WAS DUE TIME THAT THE TOWNIEST TOWNIES AND TWEENS ALIKE embraced the idea of a motivational speaker. Lethargy wasn't going anywhere, nor was the lingering sense of communal apathy. It was in every fiber of Freedom Point—the old pastel strip mall and dried-up memorial bog—like somebody left a postcard out in the sun and let the color drain and called it a town. Freedom Pointians struggled to find the energy to do much of anything in such an uninspired space, and, for that, the ancestors were mostly to blame.

WHEN THE EARLY SETTLERS FIRST PASSED THROUGH THE RUGGED territory, they had their sights set on California and a treasure known as California Rust Pipe, which, in the end, turned out to be less profitable than they'd hoped. Still, the rugged went, and sought, and found.

At least that's what the Freedom Point settlers had heard.

Their group never made it westward. The settlers missed the morning departure alarm and woke up alone in what would become Freedom Point, and, after an official unofficial vote, decided that *if it was meant to be, it would have been, so no sense in wasting effort where effort needn't be wasted*. That was the thing about adventure. It wasn't for everybody.

Settling was no cakewalk either, though. The town that the first Freedom Pointians built was really just a bunch of half-suspended tents and wooden signs that said "Dibs" in gooseberry marker. Rumor had it that some of the Rust Pipers rolled back into town and tried to help by spending all summer tilling a nearby hay field, but some sort of root mixed with the air and the sun and each and every settler caught a bad case of contagious yawn. The Rust Pipers split after that. So did the renegade Indians of Freedom Point, who chose to settle five towns over in Firecracker Village. It was a universal tragedy when they went, as they took all of the adventure with them. Handsaws. Ghost stories. Marijuana. Snakes.

THINGS ONLY GOT WORSE FROM THERE. THE MODERN FREEDOM POINT yawn took almost six seconds to complete, which happened almost one hundred times a day, which shaved hours off of the standard Freedom Point Junior High curriculum, which meant most classes only got through half a textbook, if that, which meant big trouble once statewide testing settled in town and all of Wisconsin forced Freedom Point to find a way to teach more than twelve of the fifty states.

Caffeine was supposed to be the remedy, the hero. Then intermittent air horns over the loudspeaker, too, and big rubber spiders all around the halls to shock people into staying alert or restless or scared. A nearby Chippewa casino recommended blasting the air conditioners, which led to an unfortunate case of hamster pneumonia in the science wing. Rumor had it that their babies still lived in the heated drywall.

That was the thing about hamsters. They weren't for everybody.

It was a battle against nobody but themselves in Freedom Point for quite some time, for centuries upon centuries, until somebody heard a tip from somebody five towns over about Del Calhoun, and how he turned a similar school around with his motivational pow wow—and it wasn't nothing to be afraid of, either. Just an ancient fire within his soul, a need to ignite the tired and the troubled, and it'd come out especially for corporate events, parties, weddings and etc. The fee was minimal and the result was maximal, and with two personal checks and a phone call, Freedom Point Junior High asked Del Calhoun to pass through town and inspire something or somebody.

Everybody was in good hands, if not great. Del Calhoun came from a long line of adventurers. His great great great grandfather, Chippewa Chief Shenandoah, organized the very first chili cook off in the history of the universe, so Del Calhoun had a whole bunch of ambition in his blood to share, and this is what he promised: A spiritual experience for man, woman, and child—except for babies. Those were a liability. Rejuvenation of mind, body, and soul. Focused magic. Precise psychological reboot. Perfect rebirth. Innovative inspiration. Second chance stab at greatness, and, at the very least, he had enough material to fill an entire first hour class, which was a dream come true for all students and staff of Freedom Point Junior High.

When he actually arrived this is what Del Calhoun delivered:

Overhead light flicker into total gym darkness into a tribal drum track that skipped on the Freedom Point Junior High stereo system. The lights came back up and a fair skinned man in a burlap poncho posed at center court. Streaks of face paint ran from his nose to his ears and his moccasins vibrated as he tried so hard to hold his arms out, like he was about to take flight, crouched down in an unfinished jump as the drum beat on, in and out in unsteady rhythms of technical difficulty. Still, he didn't move. Not when the beat seemed to slow or the lights jumped or an unsettling smell of electrical smoke seemed to trail out of the overhead speakers. Not even when the janitor meandered his way over to the stereo system, which he soon began hitting with a hard end of broom. The music finally cut for good and the janitor yelled.

"Which track?"

Del Calhoun kept his arms out, his knees bent, but let his head hang in disappointment before shout-whispering back.

"Track 5."

"Track 9?"

"Track. Five."

The lights fell again; the tribal beat from the beginning, this time until the end without any interruption. Lights up, again, as Del Calhoun clapped his hands and crouched even lower. Suddenly, a solid white eagle flew in from a side hallway and dropped a velvet bag near center court. It took a low lap around the gym and landed on Del Calhoun's shoulder. All of Freedom Point Junior High silently watched, mesmerized or drowsy—who could know for certain. The eagle gnawed on her own feathery breast as Del journeyed closer to the bleachers and walked the stunt off. People started to whisper at that point, young ones and teacher ones, but when Dell raised his wrists again, all of Freedom Point, Home of the Settlers, fell silent. Del let the tension linger for a moment, and then, without warning, opened his mouth and threw his arms back and let out a long, wild howl that shook the doorknobs and the basketball racks. After that, another uncomfortable silence and an equally noisy transition.

"Show of hands," he yelled. "Who's ready to chase the fire within?"

All of Settler Nation looked around, unsure of what the right answer was. It sounded dangerous, maybe wasn't worth it. No sense wasting effort where effort needn't be wasted. The velvet bag at center court wriggled a little bit on its own and the eagle flapped, but that was about it. Del Calhoun tried again with a little less risk.

"Show of hands," he said. "Who's here today? Who's just simply here?"

After a momentary hesitation, hands went up in a slow wave. First, a tentative rise from Principal McPhee at the top of the bleachers, who was recently labeled "dangerously unmotivated" by the state board. Then came the new teachers and the Sixth Graders, the ones that were almost always eager to be a part of anything, but equally afraid to show it. The popular girls came next—the Sevenths then the Eighths—and, once enough of the way was paved, the jocks followed with a certain swagger. The wannabe thugs and the inbetweeners and the weirdos came next, followed by the final group of assorted jerks, who waited just long enough to crack jokes and roll their eyes and ironically raise their hands, all of which got the eagle riled up again. Del wiggled his arm to calm her down as he praised the people of Freedom Point for at least showing up, as history proved *that even that was unreliable.*

"Well, I'm here, too, and so is Coyote," he said as she settled into her talons. "And together, we're all just dreamcatchers." Del made a rainbow with his hand on that last word and repeated it once more for anybody that missed it in the bleachers.

Somebody snickered in the top row and a few members of each representative group yawned in approval. Del pointed up on a diagonal and joined in with a startling amount of zest.

"I hear you, brother, and have I got news for you."

"I'm a girl," she said, so soft and uncomfortable it barely made it down to the floor.

"Doesn't matter," Del said, "Because boys, girls, animals, minerals, I've got news for all of you, Settlers." Del cracked his knuckles and licked his lips and squatted down, Coyote bobbing along on his shoulder. His legs nearly disappeared under his draped burlap, as his hands went up to frame his mission statement.

"If you can yawn, you can sleep, and if you can sleep, you can dream."

Coyote flapped her wings, seemingly trying to fill the deafening silence of Freedom Point unenthusiasm. Del popped back up to walk it off, the frayed edges at his waistline swaying.

"I'm not unlike you, Freedom Point. I've got dreams, too, some of them so big that I freeze in the face of adversity. But I, like you, Settler Nation, come from a long line of dreamers, and together we're going to make a pact to support one another as fellow dreamcatchers." Del stopped mid-transition and spun to face the audience. Coyote bobbled a bit before easing into a gaze on the second row.

"Is it alright *if I call you that, dreamcatchers*?" Someone in the middle let out a disappointed sigh, but nobody had the energy to openly object. Somewhere, a window must've been open, a breeze of Freedom Point dust lingering.

"Alright dreamcatchers, what I want you to do is close your eyes and I want you to think of something you want, something you really really want or really really want to be, no matter how big or small or wild it might seem." Del trailed off and smeared his tribal makeup with his hands over his eyes, covering up in a hide-and-seek stance, as everybody in the bleachers looked around. New teachers to old teachers, wannabe thugs and rumored French kiss queens. A nervous giggle glow hovered in the air.

"I'm not leaving until you're with me, dreamcatchers. I'll stay right here all night, but I'm warning you that Coyote needs to eat every few hours, and I hear she's got a taste for cooties so you'd better watch it, guys." A group of Eighth Grade girls laughed at that and covered their eyes for the sake of feeling dumb, together, which gave the Sevenths and Sixths permission to ease up as well. The teachers joined in and covered their eyes, and all the boys did, too, after it got weird just looking at each other.

"It's strange, dreamcatchers, " Del said from behind his hands, going for another practiced punch line. "I can't see a thing but I can still sense mystery meat cooking in the cafeteria." Everybody laughed at that one. Even Coyote nodded along.

"But, dreamcatchers, let me ask each and every one of you a question. More than anything in the whole wide world, I want to know what it will take to get you to embrace your wild. What is it you're holding back from? What kind of dream are you aiming to catch? Just yell it out while nobody's looking. This is a safe space of transformative thinking."

The overhead lights buzzed and somebody sneezed. Coyote flapped. Time passed. Finally, the worst of it. A real deal six-second yawn.

"Come on," Del said. "We're all here for each other, dreamcatchers. Anybody and everybody."

Another yawn, a digital watch beep. The center court velvet bag seemed to flop a little more on its own before giving up. Some sneaker rustle and an anxious sigh from the row of new teachers. The first suggestion was more of a question than anything, a mumble from the middle of the pack.

"Read more about gardening?"

"What's that?" Del asked.

"Read more. About gardening. I want to read more about gardening."

"Well, sure, all right!" Del said. "Or how about just 'try gardening.' How about that?" When nobody responded, Del peaked out through his fingers and into the audience. Everybody was huddled behind their hands except one middle-aged woman in a denim jumper with an embroidered googly-eyed banana across the neckline.

"*Wouldn't you like to just try gardening?*" he asked again. "If you can dream it, you can do it."

"Oh, I don't know," she said, still deep in thought. "My husband doesn't like for me to go outside much. Too many bees. Nature's weapons, you know." The woman slunk back behind her hands as the room fell silent again. "Let me try to think of another one," she said.

The assorted jerks cackled as the woman went through a series of ideas that all had to do with ways she could more effectively teach Home Ec. Maybe a unit on oven cleaning or a new way to watch a quiche rise. A throat cleared from somewhere down front and the wall clock seemingly started to tick slower. Coyote let out a long sigh, her eyes starting to drift off into a bird nap. Her whole body wobbled which Del took as a cue to try a new exercise.

"Change of plans," he yelled. "Maybe it's the Chippewa in me, but I like to get my feet moving and feel the earth below me." Del bent down and rubbed the palm of his hand on the gym floor, old dust and loose shoelace fuzz floating by. "I need two volunteers to help me with this next one. Just takes two dreamcatchers to help us all see what a little teamwork and risk can accomplish."

From there, two wannabe thugs volunteered to come on down after Del promised he would buy them something from the vending machine at the end of the session. The exercise was simple. One wannabe thug would say, "trust your instincts" and the other would fall and the first would catch the second and everyone would cheer because that's what trying and succeeding looked like.

Unfortunately, it was something in theory and something else in practice.

When the second thug fell, for instance, the first thug was busy asking about the vending budget, specifically the rules about Peanut M&Ms, which were significantly more expensive than the rest of the M&Ms, leaving the second thug to fall straight back on the hardwood court. Everybody gasped as he writhed in pain on the floor, rubbing all along the back of his neck.

"My collarbone," he whined. Del crouched down as Settler Nation snickering started up again.

"Is it your front or your back?"

"My back, my collarbone." The other thug started rubbing the back of his own neck, like they were connected through more than their saggy jeans and a mutual love for weaponry.

"But your collarbone's in the front," Del said. The thug curled up and hobbled to a stance as Nurse Katzler interrupted from the bleachers.

"No spoilers, please," she yelled. "Health class can only move so fast. We haven't gotten above the waist yet."

At that point, even Coyote had a hard time finding the fire within.

The danger didn't stop there, either. In a pinch, Del tried a string of other motivational tactics: a simple rejuvenation jumping jack, which sent two kids off the edge of the bleachers. A person-to-person hug that turned into a panic when two Eighth Graders got hooked on each other's earrings. A light practice in celebratory fist pumping, which led to a whole line of knuckle-to-back-of-the-head injuries.

"My collarbone," they all whined, jocks and kissers and in-betweeners rubbing their hands and heads.

Before anybody died, Del made a swift decision to call it a day. He proposed that everybody just work on finding their own spirit, on their own time, in their own controlled setting. That way, everybody could head back to regular scheduling and at least finish out the remainder of first hour. An audible gasp traveled from the top of the bleachers to the very bottom, an unparalleled panic through the whole crowd.

That was the thing about first hour. It wasn't for anybody.

"Unless," Del said. "Anybody has anything they'd like to further explore."

Everybody twisted around and made longing looks at one another, begging, pleading. When none of the Eighths or Sevenths or Sixths had the nerve to do much of anything, Principal McPhee stood up with a sudden sense of urgency. That was the thing about angry emails. They couldn't ruin his day if he avoided them.

"We should stay," he yelled. "I...I want to be a better leader and a more selfless provider. And I want to make a lot more money. In that order." He lingered, wringing his hands out as Del slowly stopped gathering his things and let out a long sigh of relief.

"Now, *there*," he said. "That's the dreamcatcher attitude. Now all you have do is brave the beast known as fear."

"I will," Principal McPhee yelled. "Yes, sure."

Del peaked behind himself at the center court velvet bag and took a moment to think. He let a single nod surface and motioned for Principal McPhee to come on down, which led to a tentative bleacher descent. On the floor, Del crossed back to the bag and hunched over as Coyote kept an eye on Settler Nation. Principal McPhee approached Del, who stayed huddled up in himself. He grunted and struggled on his knees with the bag until turning around in what seemed to be slow motion. In his hands, two plump feet of live yellow snake—the first snake in Freedom Point in nearly 400 years.

Everybody screamed in waves as Principal McPhee tried to cross back over and up to his spot, stepping on loose backpacks and illegal glass bottles.

"You can't run from the animal within," Del yelled. "Chase the fire and brave the beast!" He held his hands straight out and let the snake dangle at its core. All of the Settlers waited, wide-eyed, the most invested that they'd ever been in anything other than calling it a day in centuries. At that point, Principal McPhee only had one option.

"I make my destiny!" he yelled and Coyote screeched along. He let the snake's tongue caress his wristwatch as he took hold of its belly. Del stomped his feet and clapped his hands and wrangled all of Settler Nation with a new celebratory electricity.

"Who else wants to face fear and chase the fire?" Students' hands went up with unbelievable force and speed. Del zeroed in on the wannabe thugs first. When they started to trip their way over, Del asked for their dreams in exchange. After a brief conference, one spoke up, an ice pack on the back of his head.

"We wanna be famous and I want to try beer." All the Eighth Grade boys cheered because they, too, had heard about beer.

The wannabe thugs got grabby with their hands as Del interrupted the fanfare. He let the snake hang off to his side as he finished, Coyote perched up on the opposite shoulder.

"You guys know that if you study hard and get the math right," he said, "you can *make* beer someday." With that, the thugs nearly foamed at the mouth. They shared another brief conference before surfacing once more.

"We want to figure out decimals this year."

"Yeah, that too," the other said. "Math and stuff."

Del handed the snake over and all of Settler Nation went wild, especially when he announced that they were, in fact, certified Chippewa warriors ready for dream battle. Another group of boys followed and some Sixth Grade nobodies and a slow stream of teachers, each and every one of them thrilled to stand before the others and reclaim some long slinky line of unbridled adventure.

"I want a boyfriend and I want him to be taller."

"And you deserve it," Del said.

"I want to lose the rest of my baby teeth this year."

"Just dream them right out of their roots," Del said.

"I want to [run faster] [seem cooler] [do something that means anything to anybody]…"

"This is your beginning, dreamcatcher," Del said, passing the snake from Settler to Settler.

Halfway through the act, Coyote started flapping without command, which Del tried to ignore until she started to take off in loops towards the rafters. Del tried to coax her down with a whisper and asked everybody to cool off a little. The snake went limp, dropping to the floor and speed-slithering itself into a dusty corner. All the girls shrieked. Some of the Drama Club boys, too. Coyote hovered her way over to a basketball hoop and started getting weirder as a gentle rumble surfaced from just outside the gym, some sort of foreign snarl in the hallway, louder and louder. At that point, all of Settler Nation froze in fear—Del included. In the silence, everybody slid closer to one another, away from the hallway doors. Coyote made time to screech one last warning from up above before, in an instant, the gym doors flew open and a bobcat on a leash appeared.

On the other end, a man with golden skin and moccasins under a cattle hide poncho. On his back, a bedazzled spoon, dipping into an appliqué chili bowl.

"Who's ready to light the fire—" he yelled, his voice trailing in an Indian standoff. He eyed Del and stopped in his tracks.

"Who are you?" he said. The bobcat hissed. Coyote flapped. The snake writhed. Del Calhoun stuttered.

"I'm Del Calhoun master motivator spiritual guide extraordinaire."

He said it all together like that, and put his arms out to take flight. Coyote failed to respond to the command.

"Who are you?" Del said.

The man with the bobcat pulled the leash, a loud snarl from the other end.

"I'm Del Calhoun," he said.

Everybody in the bleachers snickered all together at that point. There was no time or space for a wave of realization. Del Calhoun, the first one, the original one that set up camp before anybody and their bobcat rolled in, started to get more worked up. He looked all around the gym for security of some kind.

"*I'm* Del Calhoun," he said, "so…you'd better change your story pal, because it's you against me and my dreamcatchers." He said the last part again for dramatic effect. He waved his arms up over his head and the whole crowd, finally, went wild on cue. Coyote did a nice big loop, dust falling from the rafters and raining down like confetti. People whistled as he went on. "Yeah, that's right, because we're all dreamcatchers and you can't stop us from chasing the night, so you'd better take your—"

"Walt?" The new Del Calhoun inched closer to Del Calhoun, a strong hold on his bobcat's neck. "You've got to be shitting me." The gym fell silent all at once, with great intent, in perfect harmony. The new Del reached his hand out and wiped a corner of Del's war paint off. "Jesus,

Walt," he said. "Is this why you took the day off?" Del avoided eye contact and stroked Coyote's head.

"No," he finally managed. "You said you didn't want the gig so I took it off the calendar, wanted to try one myself."

"Well you didn't take it off *my* calendar," New Del said. "Not that your inability to do anything is anything new." New Del put his hand on Walt's pale neck. "How many times do I have to tell you, the job takes focus and fire. You have to leave it to the pros." New Del flashed a smile and waved his hand, his bobcat nestled up to his cattle hide. "My intern Walt, everybody!"

Nobody said or did much of anything. New Del waved his hand again waiting for applause. The spirit didn't catch fire, plain and simple, which New Del took as a cue to send his assistant packing without a proper goodbye. Walt scanned the whole audience, an entire camp of fellow outsiders looking for guidance. He looked so defeated, his face long and his paint uneven as he slunk off to the side of the gym.

"Coyote, come here baby girl," New Dell yelled. "She's supposed to be at the groomer, Walt." Coyote clung to Walt's shoulder and flapped her wings, but seemingly refused to move her feet. "Coyote," New Del said, crouching down with no result. "Coyote, now." By the fourth or fifth try, he crossed over and attempted to physically pry her off, but her feet danced in the crevices of Walt's neck. People laughed, Walt included. "Everybody, settle down," he yelled. "Please, settle. Coyote. Now." Del's bobcat got crabby as he pulled her across the gym floor. "Come on, right now."

Walt tried to shake Coyote off and meet Del halfway, but when he moved, she inched all around his body, all the way across his back and down to his wrist. People clapped and cheered, which seemed to give Walt an extra kick.

"Go on Coyote," he yelled, and shook his arm out. Coyote did a full lap of the gym, swooped clear over everybody in the bleachers, grazed their hair gel and jacket shoulders and fingertips as they all reached up together and tried for a piece of her adventure. When she circled back, she landed square on Walt's shoulder again. At that point, everybody screamed with uncontrollable joy.

Del Calhoun yelled over the applause. "Stop it!" he said, trying to yank Coyote clear off Walt's shoulder. "Settle down, all of you." With that, a slow stream of booing surfaced, first from the wannabe thugs and the assorted jerks. Then the Eighth Graders, the Sevenths, the Sixths, and all between, all the way to the top of the bleachers where the teachers teamed up with Principal McPhee, who, with the *most* enthusiasm, cupped his hands around his mouth for added effect. Then came the feet stomping and the earth shaking and the coordinated chanting of Walt's name. Focused magic, plain and simple.

New Del finally snatched Coyote up while all of Freedom Point lost control.

"Get me my snake," he yelled. Walt crossed to the corner of the gym and scooped it up. It squirmed as he dusted it off, its tongue in and out to the rhythm of the people. He returned to New Del, cradling the snake like some precious vital organ, but before he handed it off, he gave one last look to Settler Nation. Young ones, teacher ones, wannabes and more. Loud and alive and ready for one final fiery dream, Walt's in particular.

The snake caught the light as he thrust it above his head.

"I want to be a motivational mastermind and I am a motivational mastermind because I own the fire and this is Freedom Point!"

With that, Walt stomped on Del's foot and took off across the floor with the snake and Coyote in tow, in his arms and on his back, straight out the side doors and off across the back lawn. Everybody lost it as Del scrambled with his bobcat and called for backup.

"Bring cages," he yelled into a flip phone.

IT DIDN'T TAKE LONG FOR THE POLICE TO FIND WALT. HE GOT TIRED OR confused while crossing the school jungle gym and set up camp underneath a swing set. By the time an officer seized the snake, it was essentially over. Settler Nation gathered around the front entrance of the school and watched the police take Walt away. Even with his hands tied, he bit two officers on the shoulders before he was finally locked into the back seat. Another officer tried to catch Coyote with a net as she swooped in and out of a school dumpster, picking up old juice boxes. Del Calhoun retreated to his own airbrushed van, a giant mural of a multi-colored flames on the side.

Right before the squad car departed, the officers cracked Walt's window so that he could say goodbye to the camp of Freedom Pointians. He struggled to crane his neck up and into the glass, his makeup smeared and lips outstretched through the top.

"Think of me from time to time and chase the fire, even when you can't find it," he yelled. "And be who you are, even if it isn't who you *are*."

Students couldn't help but cheer, teachers too. Something in their blood mixed with something from the sun that overpowered whatever remnant of ancient dust still lingered in the air. All that was left to do was to promise to be better or braver in big applause and full body wave goodbye. Coyote let out a long battle cry and followed the police car from up above as the people of Freedom Point chased after the taillights, all the way to the very edge of school grounds. Some kids looked like they might cry, but instead a wild howl took hold, some sort of new unfiltered fight.

Coyote circled back once more before heading in a brand new direction. Some swore that, as she disappeared for good, a whole stream of hamsters filed out of the science wing gutter, young ones and old ones, right out of the cozy confines of faded brick and mortar, and took off on their own trail.

That was the thing about settling. It wasn't for everybody.

Go Home, Karlee Starr

IT USUALLY DIDN'T WORK OUT BETWEEN STUDENTS AND TEACHERS AT Freedom Point Junior High, but Mr. Marbury was not the usual.

Karlee Starr wrote his name in the middle of December on her assignment notebook calendar. She drew four hearts around the y and then eventually scribbled one out. Love was crazy like that. Karlee watched the ink soak through as a long hiss surfaced from an adjacent desk.

"Gross." Tally Majors rolled her eyes and snapped her gum in time with Mr. Marbury's marker on the dry erase board. She set her gaze on Karlee's notebook, her eyes lined in glitter powder and cool girl dust.

"Have you ever even kissed a guy?" she whispered. "Because they kiss back, it's not like your hand."

Karlee set her marker down. Tally Majors was completely totally actually talking to her. *The* Tally Majors with her own gel pens, her own boyfriend, her own cell phone. Karlee tried to play it cool, pushing her chest out and playing with her ponytail before words finally escaped.

"Well actually, I am like rubber and you are like glue, so yes I have kissed someone." Tally stared in disbelief before forcing out a yawn. Karlee continued. "Are you going to Blizzard Blast?"

"If you're asking me to go, I'm not gay."

"No I'm actually like going with Mr. Marbury, so…" Tally scrunched her face up.

"No you're not," she said, "You can't dance with Mr. Marbury. Mr. Marbury doesn't go to Blizzard Blast, he *monitors* Blizzard Blast."

"I know and he asked me to monitor too," Karlee whispered back, "so it's not a big deal but it is."

When Mr. Marbury offered Karlee the position, he praised her for her undying dedication to Freedom Point Junior High, her congenial wit and warmth, her simply outstanding deconstruction of classist regulation in *Superfudge*. Or something like that.

"Karlee Starr, do you have any friends?" he said upfront, his sleeves rolled as he sat on the corner of his desk before first hour. "How many friends, if you had to guess?"

Karlee made a list in her head, starting with Aunt Donna and by association, Uncle Toby. Perhaps the two wannabe thugs who were always kind enough to ask Karlee to move before they launched mechanical pencil crossbows during Science. Then Mom and maybe Dad, if he ever decided to come back for them.

"Do parents count?" Karlee asked.

"How about this," Mr. Marbury said. "Let's just limit it to school. Do you sit alone at lunch?"

Karlee laughed in relief. "Oh no, no, that was last year. I eat with Donald Simmons now."

"Well alright then," Mr. Marbury said, standing and straightening the seat of his khakis while Karlee continued on.

"That's why I'm trying to learn sign language. So I can finally say hello."

Mr. Marbury sat back down.

"Karlee Starr," he said, "since you're so cutting edge, how about you help me out with a super special job." He lowered his voice and looked both ways in the empty classroom before continuing. "A job *nobody* has ever had because nobody was special enough until now."

Karlee's eyes grew wide as she nodded and tried not to simply combust.

"Yes," she said, "I'll do it, whatever it is, I'm there." Her eyes locked on his, a trail of saliva starting to form on the corner of her mouth. Mr. Marbury put his hands out in front of him; his palms covered in dry erase graffiti as he cleared his throat and stretched two words into a lifetime.

"Blizzard. Blast."

Then Mr. Marbury turned and pulled a single rose from underneath a stack of *Rumble Fish* essays, fog drifting in from the hallway. It was the absolute most perfect moment. He spoke.

"Karlee," he said. "Karlee," louder.

Karlee swallowed her spit and returned to real time, the classroom fogless.

"You good?" Mr. Marbury asked, his hand on the shoulder of her sweatshirt.

"Perfect," she whispered.

"So I have to go tomorrow night, right, to make sure everyone has a super special time, right? Well I was thinking that maybe *you* could come to the dance and *you* could help *me* by being a super special student...well, a student...monitor. Yes, a *monitor*, so you can keep an eye on everyone in case I'm busy with something else. Because my job as monitor is really busy, but I'm sure I don't have to explain that to someone as cutting edge as you, right?"

Karlee shook her head *no*, her hand in her mouth adjusting a gold orthodontic rubber band.

"And maybe just maybe," Mr. Marbury added, "We can have our own special signals that only monitors get. Like I can touch my nose if everything's clear or I can tug my ear if I need backup. That way, we don't have to talk all night. Because," he tacked on, "I wouldn't want to disturb your super special job."

Karlee tried to think of men more honorable in that moment and came up short.

"So…" Mr. Marbury said. "We have a deal?"

Students began filing in the room as Karlee beamed in backwards steps to her desk and began filling a square with purple Sharpie. She drew the curves of Mr. Marbury's name until Tally Majors took a seat and tested her credibility.

"Mr. Marbury doesn't go to Blizzard Blast," she said, "he *monitors* Blizzard Blast."

"I know," Karlee said, "and he asked me to monitor too, so it's not a big deal but it is." Tally Majors rolled her eyes.

Karlee retraced the fourth heart in her notebook, replaying the exchange over and over on a loop for the rest of first hour. Then second. Then third through eighth, each hour the wink moving progressively slower. During ninth hour, Nurse Katzler showed a PowerPoint on the hazards of tanning beds, so Karlee allowed herself to rehearse what she might say when Mr. Marbury finally asked to be her boyfriend.

THE WAITING WAS THE HARDEST PART. KARLEE HAD WAITED TWO YEARS and twelve days for his proposal. It started in Sixth Grade, when she skinned her knee during the Honor Roll picnic after two wannabe thugs stole hand soap from the bathroom and smeared it on the cafeteria ramp. Everybody laughed real loud when Karlee dropped a plate full of beans until Mr. Marbury yelled "People! People!" and pulled her up by the elbow. He smiled real big and then Karlee smiled real big and then Mr. Marbury smiled even bigger.

"Cool rubber bands, I like those braces," he said. "Gold is the new black." Karlee ran her fingers over her two front teeth and blushed. She tried real hard not to burn from the inside out.

"Color is the new color," she said in monotone, gazing into his eyes. Mr. Marbury turned and walked away, and when he did, the air smelled like shower gel and angel whispers. In Seventh Grade, Mr. Marbury played a funny song about grammar on guitar in the Freedom Point Variety Show and Karlee couldn't sleep for two weeks straight. When Karlee was switched from Mrs. Jarvis to Mr. Marbury for Eighth Grade English, she almost needed to be hospitalized. It was the absolute most perfect way to fall in love.

Of course, when he proposed, she wouldn't talk about any of those things. Instead, she would just say "yes." "Yes" she would say, a single word that would ignite a running clock on their undying love, "Yes" at 13, and he would squeeze her body so hard that she might grow an inch or two. "Yes" at 14 when Principal McPhee asked if rumors were true and "Yes" at 15 when Karlee's mom made Mr. Marbury swear to drive slow and keep an eye on her retainer. "Yes" at 17, when Mr. Marbury would ask on one knee in a city far away from Freedom Point.

"Yes," she would say, "I love you more than anyone has ever loved anything ever."

"And I love you," he would say, "You are every color of the rainbow."

At 18, the wedding would be beautiful because Karlee would finally be old enough to wear a strapless dress and stay out past 10:30 and wear mascara that she would have to fix when Mr. Marbury whispered "You won't be alone again."

Yes, that is how it would all begin and end and begin again.

Karlee rearranged the words in her mind for the rest of the afternoon. She mouthed out phrases on the bus ride home and carved a heart into the waxy leather seat in front of her. She thought about packing a suitcase for a quick getaway while two wannabe thugs pulled the bus windows down past the black bar and got scolded. All the kids whispered with their friends while the bus driver yelled into the rear view mirror. Karlee worried about what Tally said about kissing.

When she got home, she left her backpack in the recycling bin and got ready to run away into the sunset. She put photos of herself on the fridge for her mom, and put two pairs of shoes in a cardboard box and taped it up to be shipped away, and then took a break to write in her diary about the whole event. At dinner, she got misty while listening to her mom talk about her new online boyfriend and how he might like to fly in for a weekend when the time was right.

They could all be very happy, mom and Karlee and Mr. Marbury and SausageKing69.

In the bath, Karlee worried that the rest of the body wash might go to waste and halfway through the night, she worried about getting more orthodontic rubber bands, and if she could find a way to ship her hermit crabs once things settled down. When the alarm clock went off the next morning, Karlee took the batteries out and put all the parts into the box. Then she put the rest of the day in there too: Mr. Marbury's final lecture as her teacher. Coach Drews' stupid gym class tennis shoe rule. Lunch tray fruit cocktail in heavy syrup. Egyptian Pyramids Chapter 7. Nurse Katzler's mug collage of her husband and her poodle. Two wannabe thugs running shirtless through the hall. Karlee put it all away when she got home and readied herself to be somebody else.

By 6:00, Karlee had tried on two dozen outfits. She settled on a white velvet leotard with a white denim skirt that she found tucked away in her mom's closet. Then she cut the fingers off her old shoveling gloves and craft glued sequins all over them. She laid the ensemble on her bedspread while she ran her hands through a Caboodle full of expired makeup that Aunt Donna gave her when dad left with PJ Sotheby's mom. The plastic box was divided into sandwich bags that Aunt Donna labeled either "Daytime" or "Sex," which Karlee covered in Lisa Frank stickers with no particular system in mind. Seated at her bedroom desk, she unzipped a sandwich bag labeled with six neon dolphins and pulled out a half-used eye shadow, lining the base of her eyebrows in royal blue with her fingertips. Gradually filling the arches of both eyes, Karlee checked herself in the Caboodle mirror insert before she licked her hands and smeared the excess blue on to the leg of her desk. She fished a lipstick out of the same sandwich bag and outlined her mouth in a waxy red before pulling all of her hair to the right side of her head and securing the mess with a rubber band. Karlee played with the ends of her ponytail as she crossed back to her bed and began to change. She considered stuffing the top of her leotard with tissue or orphaned socks but when she tried it, she looked like she was shoplifting a teddy bear. Instead, Karlee worked on conversation starters to compensate for any shortcomings.

"Do you come here often?" she said with a forced smoky husk.

Zipping her skirt and re-teasing her pony, she retreated back to the Caboodle mirror for one final look. With all of the makeup, she barely recognized herself. It was beautiful.

Karlee grabbed her sneakers from the closet and headed for the door as her mom called up from the bottom of the staircase. At the light switch, she paused for a moment and gave her bedroom one last look. The purple walls. The zebra border. A Tiger Beat spread on Paolo Sonata tacked up above her headboard in sequential order. A mint shag rug and a tropical tank. Up top, a soccer participation trophy and a Beanie Baby enclosed a plastic cube. Two pictures with mom's other boyfriends. A used-up band-aid from the Sixth Grade picnic. Karlee listened to her hermit crabs rearrange neon stones as she lingered. She tried to feel sad or meaningful or wise, but she couldn't. There was simply too much to look forward to.

THE GYM SMELLED LIKE BUBBLEGUM AND FACE WASH WHEN KARLEE arrived. Somebody fashioned a big polar bear out of construction paper and taped it up over the mural of the Freedom Point Memorial Bog. A blue strobe light cut real time in half as Karlee searched the floor, her coat draped over her arm and her full body glowing beneath a black light. The basketball hoop had a single streamer hanging from the rim and Karlee watched it shake to the bass of a club track until a pair of hands waved from the makeshift stage above the dance floor. Mr. Marbury smiled and gave a thumbs up while the DJ nodded along. Karlee waved back and waited under the hoop. She folded her coat into a compact square and tried to remember all of the absolute most romantic things she thought she might like to say.

Mr. Marbury disappeared into the crowd before crossing the court. He straightened his tie as he approached Karlee on the very edge of the gym. She massaged her hair as he got closer, and when he got closest, he put his hand out for a firm handshake. His skin felt like warm biscuit and magic spell. As he squeezed, he leaned to the left and held one hand up in an eager wave to somebody in the distance. Karlee turned her head and looked out the gym door. Nurse Katzler was waving back, smiling extra wide from the hallway. Karlee smiled and waved, too.

"A real saint, that woman!" Mr. Marbury yelled into Karlee's ear. He leaned in closer. "She's always on the clock. Last year, two kids drank glow sticks. You just never know, do you?"

Karlee put her hands up and laughed real loud so that he knew she knew it was a joke. Mr. Marbury leaned in again and yelled into Karlee's ear.

"You look really pretty tonight," he said. "I'm glad you came, Karlee Starr."

"I love you," she yelled back.

"What's that?" he yelled.

"I said…I said I am too."

Mr. Marbury lunged backwards and tapped his nose and tossed her a wink.

"I'm gonna take a walk around and make sure everything's okay" he yelled, Karlee Starr nodding to the music. "And if anything gets out of control, you come find me okay?" Karlee continued to nod. "And one more thing."

Karlee Starr, like a metronome.

"Relax, Karlee Starr." Mr. Marbury put his hands on her shoulders and swayed her to the music before backing away. He grooved his way out with his arm extended towards Karlee's face, which she covered with her bedazzled gloves to keep fireworks from coming out. It was the absolute most perfect romantic exchange.

Karlee shook her limbs as Mr. Marbury disappeared across the floor and towards the bathrooms. She took a seat on the bleachers to collect herself, and watched her peers in the wild. Two girls from Karlee's math class took photos of themselves with a digital camera while two boys stood in the background making lewd gestures. The DJ told Tally Majors to leave room for the Holy Ghost during "The Locomotion." An Eighth Grade couple slow danced, then broke up, and then slow danced again to a Whitney Houston song. All the girls cried to Taylor Swift. And Ben Bertram and some of the boys from Drama Club. When two lunch ladies brought out a vat of Gatorade, everyone got rowdy, blue stains down their shirts and skirts and piles of Dixie cups jammed into crevices of the bleachers. Karlee picked up all the cups. She organized them by the color of lip gloss on the rim. Then she counted how many kids crushed the cups and how many didn't. Then she sat on the floor and waited for Mr. Marbury to come back. She watched the clock for fifteen minutes. Then she watched kids come and go from the bathrooms, one group after another. Then she counted songs, and chewed her nails, and played with her hair until she couldn't think of anything else to do.

After a group of nosy parents arrived exceptionally early, Karlee took a walk through the main hallway, and started to stress out about the pressure of the wedding and the move and everything. It was all so important. She worried that she might have to plan it alone, that Mr. Marbury might've disappeared altogether, because sometimes things happened like that. She worried that she might die of anxiety before he returned, and then he might die of loneliness. It would be so romantic if one died saving the other, and it would be even more romantic if she was 'the other.' But then, how great would it be to die at the very exact same time. Now that would be—

Karlee stopped planning and froze mid-step in the hallway, zeroing in on a nearby rustling. The main hallway was empty except for the glow of a single light from Nurse Katzler's office. The rustling happened again, louder, as Karlee Starr moved towards the light. She tried to think of who could possibly be on the exam table if nobody left the gym under her watch. Unless of course…it was the only other option. The only other instance that could possibly explain the mumbling and movement of two separate bodies in that office:

A burglar.

Karlee fixed her ponytail, her body hot in anticipation. It was the absolute most perfect romantic way to die, to be shot by a burglar, to be buried as a hero. She crept her way towards the scene, her marshmallow feet in soft steps en route to the door. She covered one tile at a time and counted down, closer and closer until she crouched beneath the office doorknob. The DJ told everyone to put their hands in the air in the gym as Karlee bent her knees and got ready to pounce. She said a little prayer and asked God to let Mr. Marbury move on after her death. Then she asked God to keep her alive enough to get at least one full body hug. The office rustling picked up and Karlee took a deep breath, before leaping up as fast as she could to face the door. She peered in through the slim window. Her arms fall to her sides. She didn't move. Didn't punch. Or bleed. Or run or kiss or anything. Her heart slowed to a stop.

There they were. There he was. Him.

Standing with his knees against hers, running his hands through *her* hair, *her* weight on *her* palms on the paper of the exam table. Karlee struggled to get her eyes and her brain to connect. It looked like Mr. Marbury was drying Nurse Katzler's chest off, but instead of using a towel, he used the buttons on the front of his shirt. Nurse Katzler showed a lot of bra, and not just the straps. Mr. Marbury looked for something with his hands on the inside of her skirt. He looked like he was in pain. Karlee thought about opening the door to help him find whatever he was looking for, but before she could make up her mind, Nurse Katzler whispered something in his ear and he started to laugh.

Karlee tried to move away from the window, but spent all of her energy on trying not to cry. She counted ceiling tiles and bit her tongue and tried to listen to the DJ leading the limbo down the hall. She swallowed hard, her whole body drenched in an unfamiliar sadness as she imagined what it might be like to not have to imagine anymore.

Then she started to cry.

She cried because her insides stopped working and nobody even cared enough to shoot her when she so desperately needed to be shot. She got louder and a high-pitch whimper made its way out from where her heart used to be. She hadn't cried so hard since the time that Tally and her friends told her about Santa not being real.

A lonely whistle surfaced from some empty space deep inside, loud enough to bounce right off the walls and back into her chest. In the office, Mr. Marbury slowed down as he tried to locate the source of the whimper. Karlee tried to quiet as she watched him watch the ceiling for movement—Nurse Katzler curled up into herself—but as soon has he caught a glimpse of the tragedy at the door, he slipped into a panic. Karlee stood real still and tried to be invisible, and when it didn't work, she started choking on her spit, which was, in fact, the absolute very least romantic way to die. She covered her eyes with her gloves and tried to sprint in six different directions at once. The DJ dared everybody to slow dance. In the hallway, Karlee hyperventilated and gave up and sat down. Mr. Marbury took a knee and put a hand on her shoulder. His breath got real heavy and he spoke real low, slowly.

"Karlee," he said. "Did I ever tell you how special you are?"

Melted eyeshadow dripped on the hallway tile as she hung her head. After a moment of silence and distant Boyz II Men, pastel makeup smeared the backs of her gloves as she wiped her eyes. Without looking up, she spoke in broken gasps.

"I-love-you," she said. "You are every color of the rainbow and I love you."

Mr. Marbury froze. He took a deep breath and stood up and backed away. He rubbed his forehead and almost started to say something that looked a lot like something Karlee didn't want to hear.

It didn't look anything like going somewhere better or brighter, or having a full family again with mom and mom's new boyfriend. Karlee looked up and cleared her throat and calmed a bit. She readied herself to say it all again, but when she opened her mouth, a piercing buzz interrupted.

Mr. Marbury put his hands up in surrender and looked for smoke and Karlee put her gloves on her ears. Nurse Katzler whipped the office door open and took off without a left shoe. Mr. Marbury pulled Karlee up off the ground but it didn't feel like the absolute most perfect gesture.

The rhythm of the alarm continued, an overhead light flashing hazards twice as they both looked down the hallway to gym. Two wannabe thugs made a mad sprint towards them and laughed. They both stopped, one with a handful of used cigarettes.

"Aw shit," he said. The other pulled him by the sleeve and they sprinted into an adjacent bathroom. Mr. Marbury took off in a slow jog after them.

"Wait," Karlee yelled. He turned towards her as he continued to jog backwards. "I love you," she said. He stopped and wiped his face with his hands, his eyes rolled back. He shook his head.

"Go home, Karlee Starr."

Karlee watched Mr. Marbury dodge a door down the hall as kids stampeded from the gym, the alarms still buzzing. The jocks cleared the door first and practiced proper form on the way out. Three girls cried. And some of the Drama Club boys. A group of Seventh Graders ran by, drenched in sweat and spicy cologne. Sixth Graders got pushed while triple-checking leather sleeves for their parents' digital cameras. Tally Majors stopped and wobbled and puked neon blue in a nearby trashcan. The DJ stopped to hand out business cards by the L-P locker bank. Abandoned strobe lights made shadows on the hallway walls as Karlee felt the breeze of her peers disappear. It was the absolute most lonely place to be.

The wannabe thugs were the last to leave, all tangled up in a joint sprint as authorities arrived, and Mr. Marbury surfaced shortly after. He stood there in the hall, and Karlee stood there too, but it was uncomfortably clear that they weren't standing there together. He barely even looked at her, much less said anything about anything. Karlee waited for some sort of apology—for leaving so fast or fleeing at all—but when it never surfaced, she finally took things into her own hands. She crossed the divide, tile by tile, inching her way to the other side of the hall. There, she reached out and took hold and hugged Mr. Marbury without any intention of letting go. An emergency light flashed, a noisy buzz still ringing. Mr. Marbury tried to shake her off a few times, tried to make an exit as a fire truck rumbled its way onto school grounds, but when she swayed with his body, he simply started walking with her attached to his chest.

Somewhere, there was romantic fog, a single rose. Maybe a strapless dress. A wedding, a sunset, a new home, too, but, until then, Karlee held on tight and lingered in the heat of an imaginary fire.

The Wilderness

WHEN THE HUNTERS INVADED TROPICAL CHERRAPUNJI, HALF OF THEM brought pornography. Most of the men favored Brazilian waxes and names like "Jasmine." The women of the pack carried old Harlequins, old issues of *Playgirl* where Leonardo DiCaprio used words like "passion" next to "iceberg." Two of the women bonded over Leo on page 75, soft lighting and cotton tunic nothingness. The men bonded over a latex co-ed holding a chainsaw, but skin was skin was skin. Man, woman, waxed, bearded, airbrushed, 80's, 90's—all of it made the same firecracker rattle in the tropical rain, sopping copies of old magazines. The porno-enthusiasts knew it well, faded four-letter words in ink on their fingertips as they held their issues up in the tropical downpour—waiting, alone, together.

Every so often, someone would flip a page, hoping a new angle of a tit or dick might lure more than a happenstance bird out of the wilderness. Other hunters used different bait. Some yelled obscene curse words into the air. Some chewed their nails and spit the tips on the ground. Others kissed each other—loud and hard like a high school production of *Romeo & Juliet*—hard, loud, and wet, gasping for air in the endless rainfall. The really devoted kissers tried groping and nibbling.

All of the kissers were married, but not to each other. That's what made their practice so valuable, so exciting. They were smart to choose a vice that constantly evolved. Others weren't so fortunate. The nail biters quickly ran out of material. So did the pornographers for that matter.

Skin was skin was skin, no matter how you dressed it up.

Still, in the perpetual darkness of Cherrapunji summer, the hunters invaded by the dozens, setting up makeshift nylon tents and waiting—alone, together—to snap a single photograph of the ultimate prize—the yeti.

For years, people mistook the yeti for a cold weather animal, hovering over a branch bowl of glowworms in the arctic tundra, until Jessica Sanchez of Rancho Cucamonga took the very first portrait in Cherrapunji at twilight. After two divorces and a screening of *Eat, Pray, Love*, Sanchez set out on her own wanderlust and took one too many lefts on an unmarked trail. By lunchtime, she raised her knapsack and started bargaining with God.

"Lord," she said, "If you shall take me, let me leave this Earth as pure as I arrived."

By nightfall, Sanchez changed her tune.

"Fuck you," she muttered, her face in her bag. "Not like you even exist." She shook a cigarette out of the bottom, the rainfall beading on the back of her neck, and found a lighter to finish the job. Branches broke as she huddled into herself, blowing smoke into a paperback copy of *Human Being or Being Human?* Motherfucking waste of time. Motherfucking soul retreat. Motherfucking Paul and Steve, motherfucking babysitters. Motherfucking loneliness. No more make-it-better, quick-fix-uplifting-quote. Loneliness. Loud and clear. Loneliness.

She lit another two cigarettes, and let the smoke seep out and mix with the rain. When the moment vanished, the figure appeared.

White fingers, white arms, white eyebrow beds. Breathing down comforter. White feet. Tufted tower of soaking wet fur. He inched closer and reached for her mouth. He smelled like something ancient and fresh, like charcoal grill and antique furniture. The rain stopped mid-air as his fur brushed her lip, a drip drip dripping of drool leaking out of his mouth. He filled his chest up with air and huffed, and in one slow swipe, he pushed all the limp cigarettes out of her mouth. She managed a single whisper as he turned to leave.

"Fuck."

The yeti circled back and surveyed her mouth again. He put a single finger to her lips and shook his head. No. The universal language. Loud and clear. He seemed to linger for her response.

"Sorry," she said. "*Fudge.*" The yeti nodded and turned to leave again, a slow creep, hunched and silent. Sanchez fumbled with her knapsack as he disappeared, eyes wet and wide. Her hands got busy in her bag, feeling her way to the lens of her camera, fishing it out as he stopped to clean his ear.

"Fuck," again, a little louder. The yeti turned back to a flash flash flash. Birds took flight and greenery shook as he instantly disappeared, so fast he simply vanished. The rain picked back up, the smell disappeared. Sanchez began to weep, loud and brand-new, shrill and piercing, until a group of nighttime yogis stumbled upon her experience.

THE PHOTOGRAPH WAS BLURRY AT BEST, BUT THE UNION OF YETI Hunters all took a look at the shadowy figure—the long white fur, the empty gaze—and agreed that it was, in fact, a certified yeti. A week later, Jessica Sanchez sold her photo to the Smithsonian for five million dollars.

"He feeds on vices," she told *Big Game Weekly*. "He's a mother-fudging vice eater and he's waiting for his next meal, somewhere." And so they went, the amateur hunters, in droves to Cherrapunji, hoping to also lure the yeti out with their own terrible habits. Maybe this time he'd even pose.

A GROUP OF ALCOHOLICS ARRIVED FIRST, BUT THEY ALL WANDERED away during an argument about the Steve Miller Band. The Ivy League cheaters came next and copied each other's tents. Then came the narcissists, the thieves, and the people who hit squirrels on the highway on purpose. Everybody brought something inexplicably terrible to share. Trixie McPhee brought a box of Tootsie Rolls.

"Sometimes, I just eat ten of these a day," she said, two fellow hunters listening begrudgingly, a spread-eagle photo of Pamela Anderson in the air. Trixie mastered the art of yelling over the rain in the first five minutes, her whole body amplified under a see-through umbrella. She held up two Tootsie Roll wrappers and the hunters continued nodding. Everything she said, she really said.

"I just can't quit 'em! I'm just about as guilty as they come, just a good ol' case of gluttony." She yelled the second part a little louder, her eyes shifting to a patch of heavy greenery. Nothing surfaced. "God came to me in a dream once and he told me to quit the stuff, no more sweets, y'know? That's why I don't go to church no more." The rain fell a little harder. Trixie ate another piece of candy and started singing a Dolly Parton song to pass the time. She was the first person to bring a true southern drawl to Cherrapunji, the first to bring a clear gingham poncho, the first to keep her face done up in the downpour, the first to give everyone a goodnight hug—even the squirrel killers. Trixie was also the first to bring a spouse, who manned his own box of Tootsie Rolls.

"If you think I'm bad, you should see David! Can barely keep paws off the stuff. Would rather see a chocolate mousse in a bikini than me, I'm sure of it!" Trixie giggled and leaned into the poncho beside her, umbrella rain spilling over. David wiped the water off and nodded and flashed a smile, his teeth covered in a brown film of sugar spit. Maybe if the yeti surfaced by midnight, he wouldn't have to eat another damn candy again.

THE LYING FIRST STARTED WHEN DAVID MARRIED TRIXIE. SHE LOOKED so sweet that love seemed secondary. Just a word, really. If it was love that she wanted to feel, David was happy to touch her—in high school under the bleachers, in college on the library lawn, at her parents over Christmas, when the underwear finally came off. Maybe it was love, whatever it was, though David never thought of her that way. Lovely, of course, which is really about the same. At the end of the day, it was David's mother that truly loved Trixie, and David truly loved David's mother, so it all really made sense. So kind, so sweet, so young, both Mama and Trixie. Then the baby happened.

Trixie's belly didn't show but David showed up anyways, at her grandma's trailer on Christmas Eve, a ring on loan from Trixie's Aunt Zelda. David told Trixie it was a sapphire because maybe it was, who would really know.

"Anything's a sapphire if you really believe it is," Aunt Zelda said.

Trixie squealed and cried and kissed and Mama helped her plan the wedding. A simple Mass and apple crisp. Carnation cross on the getaway car. Mama's satin wedding gown. She stayed up late on Sunday nights and sewed the skin right off her fingertips. It was worth it once the dress went down the aisle. Trixie looked so sweet, so young, so easy to please in old cream lace. Strawberry blonde and freckled and fresh, just like Mama before dad went and ruined it. At the end of the ceremony, David took a break from rubbing Trixie's belly and gave Mama a kiss goodnight.

"Beautiful," he said. Mama held him tight and whispered back.

"Yes," she said. "And this time for good."

THE HOLIDAYS PASSED AND TRIXIE DIDN'T GROW. ON VALENTINE'S DAY, she admitted she made the whole thing up, except the part where she said I love you. Maybe because she dreamt about a baby happening, maybe because she swore she felt something in her insides. Maybe because she wanted Mama as her own, so she could finally know what it's like to shop with one. Maybe because she wanted David forever, and didn't know how to ask for herself. Before David had a chance to really think it all over, Trixie asked if she could at least keep the ring. She looked so sad, so sweet, so lonely—so much like Mama when Dad stopped trying for good. Maybe even sadder. It was so pure, so simple. David stayed and gave and felt good doing it. He gave her a hug because it seemed right. Trixie had a hard time letting go.

"I'll never take another thing," she said.

*

THE FABERGE EGG WAS TRIXIE'S FIRST SPLURGE, AFTER THE DENTIST told her she needed a root canal and she dreamt that she'd die in the chair. David said she could have it, whatever it was, because it gave her peace of mind and things were good and she was good and that's really all that mattered. Soon after, Trixie skipped the middleman and charged up cards in David's name for almost everything. Porcelain angels. Golf clubs. She bought a lot of things for Mama, but then borrowed them indefinitely. A knife set. A sad clown painting.

She earned a rare Elvis bust when David took a school job in Freedom Point and they were forced to leave Charleston for northern Wisconsin. A series of gifts were packed and unpacked. Alligator suitcase. Aromatherapy plunger. Egyptian cotton whatever. When David was named Principal, Trixie sent all the teachers at Freedom Point Junior High designer popcorn balls for lunch. When David called to call her lovely, she informed him that she bought two cemetery plots back in Charleston because she had a dream she died of boredom and, even as a ghost, longed to be back in South Carolina, where home is *really* home.

"How much of your middle name do you want on your tombstone?"

It was always something. Trixie would sit and buy and cover herself in David—sweater sets and designer pasta he had forgotten to give her for something or other. When she found out a baby could never come, a catalogue of timeshare condos arrived in the mail. David made it disappear the following morning.

One time, Trixie admitted that all she wanted was an ostrich coat so that she'd know what it really felt like to be wealthy before she, god forbid, *actually* died.

"And the website says it's func-tion-al, too."

The coat came twice, in two different shades of eggshell.

David tried to tell Trixie no, all the time, every day, but he couldn't stand the idea of disappointing her. She'd worked so hard to stay so lovely, to keep her face so fresh over the years, so bright eyed and cheek blush like the makeup Mama did on their wedding day. She was a permanent reminder of the promise that he made. He had never even seen her cry, couldn't even imagine what that would look or sound or feel like, couldn't stand the idea of her sitting on the stoop like Mama, waiting for dad to get back and apologize. If that was honesty or love or whatever, who needed it?

Work got longer as money got tighter. Freedom Point students got worse, or so it seemed. One of them tried to set the annual dance on fire, or so it seemed. All of them went wild in one way or another and everybody had to lend a hand. David supervised extracurriculars that nobody should ever have to supervise. Gingerbread Club. Touch Soccer Team. Junior Cheese Sculptors of America. He tried so hard to seem interested in everything, all the curds and the "ankle sprains," and the hope that maybe all the bills might figure themselves out if nobody ate breakfast or snacks. Then he'd go home and a taxidermy gator would be waiting in the garage. The house felt smaller, the truth less frequent. David got tired. The tipping point was Trixie's fortieth birthday where she told all of her friends that they were buying a condo in Aspen. She held up a catalogue that had garbage stains on it. David put a freeze on all the accounts without saying anything, and Trixie did the same, but with David's lower-region. A week went by and nobody said or did anything about either matter. Trixie spent the whole weekend on the phone with Mama to make a point, and the following Monday, Mama died from stress or something equally terrible. At the wake, Trixie finally opened up. She looked so sweet, so broken, so lost. It was only natural after Mama gave her so much. Trixie squeezed David tight near an old bowl of nuts on the funeral mantle. She could barely compose herself to get out everything that she needed to say.

"I can't believe it all," she said. "And to think, I was just tellin' her about how unfair you were with the condo and whatnot." Trixie wiped her nose across an ostrich sleeve as David tried to think of anything to say. Trixie filled the silence. "I guess we'll never know what finally did her in." She went on to speculate about how much they might inherit until it was clear that things were finally over.

*

TIME WAS OF THE ESSENCE. DAVID DELAYED ACTION UNTIL THE END OF the school quarter, and had some stranger five towns over drew up papers during the All-State Blue Cheese Conference. The plan was to leave them on the kitchen counter and then simply vanish for a few weeks of summer and hope she found her way back south. Maybe he could even help her move once she cooled down. That would be a good way to end the papers, a little note or joke about heavy lifting. Maybe a doodle, too. And maybe they'd go best with a nice card or box of candy— something that fit into her new all-nougat diet. Zero confrontation. Very kind. He'd even thought of a lot of nice things to say in email in case she needed them. She wouldn't be alone forever, just for a little while, and he could still come over and listen to her sometimes-psychic dreams. He'd help her paint the condo if she ever got one. Maybe it wouldn't be so bad; maybe she knew it was all coming.

When David got home from leaving, Trixie was sitting on the front stoop, waiting—two alligator suitcases on either side. Maybe she had a dream and already called her own lawyer. As David pulled in, she waved for the car to stop and dragged the bags to the passenger's side. As she got closer, she looked happier. It was not the face of a knowingly abandoned woman.

"Where'd you go?" she said.

David's voice went up an octave or two. "Students or something." He'd have to serve the papers soon if that was the best of his lying abilities.

"Oh. Well I got you somethin'," she said, a newspaper rolled up under her armpit. She shook it out and flipped to the inside, her eyes peeled back with excitement. She probably bought the paper, the whole thing, the machines and everything. She pulled a section out and handed it through the car window. The photograph was blurry at best. A shadowy figure, a handsome reward. Two flights and a camping pack. No refunds.

"We're rich!" she said. "I can feel it this time!" Trixie nearly frothed at the mouth. "Let's go get a yee-ti." She disappeared from the window, the suitcases zipping and unzipping. David tried to think of a way to let her down without actually letting her down. Maybe he'd get lucky and spontaneously die.

"Maybe the paper's old. I think I heard the story last month. Yeah. Maybe they made a mistake. We'd better go inside and just wait until we know for sure." The zippers stopped moving and Trixie popped back up. Her face softened, lengthened if possible.

"I already got the tickets." She took a big breath, more than anybody needs. "I guess I thought you'd wanna spend more time with me." She pouted and David felt instantly guilty. Maybe he could just go to the airport and then find a way to hide. Maybe the bathrooms had a trap door.

Trixie leaned in further through the window, her chest rising and falling and her eyes welling up. She took a big breath and lowered her voice.

"Plus, I wasn't gonna say anything," she said, "but I had another dream." She stopped to build suspense. "Mama says hello."

David's breath felt short. She'd probably come by to finally say I love you.

"What else did she say?"

"Well, she said that this is our chance to get the money—*real money*—and she really wants us to do it because life's too short and life is expensive and God forbid one of us dies, too, then what would we do then?" Trixie choked back tears and took David's hand. "She said she'd never ask you to do another thing. And then she died. Again."

David felt the burn of the legal envelope in his back pocket. Mama looked so helpless on Trixie, so pure, so soft white knit and cotton blend, so carnation cross and distant church bells.

He tried his hardest to make his mouth say no. He tried to finally get away for the first and last time as quietly as possible, until Trixie started making a sniffling noise. She set her gaze on David and tempted him to listen. It was so gentle, so distinct. It was nearly identical to the one Mama made when David first proposed.

"You do her right," she had said, long streams of mixed emotions rolling down her cheeks. "And when it's hard, you do it for me."

Somewhere distant, Mama probably readied herself to die again of sheer disappointment. She probably regretted spending so much time teaching Trixie how to tease her hair, how to frost a Bundt, how to make those eyeliner lines so straight. She probably regretted ever believing that David was something other than his daddy. She'd probably make the lace gown simply evaporate from earth, like socks do in the drying machine. That way, nobody else would ever have to wear it and pretend like maybe miracles happen.

David let the weight of it all vibrate through his body while Trixie kept herself busy by folding up the newspaper. She tried so hard, her hair so high, her eyes so straight. She looked so familiar in a brand new way. David watched her fingers move and felt the back-pocket papers virtually disappear before he finally interrupted.

"Okay," he said. "Let's try."

THE CHERRAPUNJI RAIN FELL THE HARDEST WHEN THE McPHEES first arrived. All the tents circled up beneath the long palm leaves on the edge of the clearing, and the hunters started mingling with each other. The kissers took a vote and started adding triple kissing into their curriculum. The cheaters played trivia with the squirrel killers, and, naturally, always won. The thieves took a liking to Trixie after she showed them her jewelry box. David wandered about the woods alone, burying little mounds of Tootsie Rolls he simply couldn't bring himself to stomach. That was all Trixie could think of when she had to pick a bad habit to pursue. Tootsie Rolls.

God bless her for trying. David wasn't nearly as good at it. He almost called the whole trip and the whole life off after Trixie spent ninety dollars on honey-glazed airport walnuts before asking him when he thought Mama's money might finally come through. She asked again during take off and when the cola cart came by and when the woman in the next row over cried during some in-flight special on what really causes sunsets. At one point, Trixie fell asleep into the crevice of David's neck and somewhere over the ocean, he let himself imagine which fellow passenger might be able to take better care of her. When the cola cart came by again, David made a list of all the things that he could say to get somebody else on board with Trixie. Semi-psychic. Smells nice. Well-kept face. Kind to both animal and child. Medically unable to bear either, but able to embody both in extreme emotional circumstances. She could be a millionaire in no time, depending on the yeti hunt. Now that was a sell. The million would definitely do it. She could probably get somebody even nicer than David with that. Better hair, even, and all it'd take was one photograph at twilight. Ten seconds and David could be a hero all over again. Mama could finally be proud, wherever she was. Maybe Trixie could be okay, too.

The sun set for good in the next row over as David found his way into finding his way out. The plan was really a three-part process. Scope out the wild of Cherrapunji and get a feel for the landscape. Cover himself in leaves or toucan dung or something equally rugged and ambush the beast. Board a flight back home and hand Trixie the camera and say "This is for you, now give me my last name back" and Trixie would say "Thank you, I forgive you, and I'm sorry about all of the gingerbread windows you were forced to measure" and everything would be so sweet and kind and sort of silly, and the papers would practically sign themselves. Mama would probably materialize for a last minute word of wisdom. Zero confrontation, no tears, no disappointment. Cherrapunji would be a place of great relief.

A KOALA ATE DAVID'S WATCH WITHIN THE FIRST HOUR OF HUNTING, but other than that, things were all right. Trixie only asked about Mama's money once or twice. The rain was warm and the boots dry as he wandered through the greenery alone and enjoyed the silence. Every so often a branch would break, another hunter crossing paths with a flashlight and a centerfold. A foreign howl surfaced from behind an old mossy log, but when David approached, it was just two kissers. They were so alive, just as exotic as a shaggy beast. He wandered by a few more times to watch, and hoped Trixie's next husband would get a piece of that.

When the kissers caught on, David snuck away to an old clearing and fished the envelope out of his back pocket. One of the thieves was so kind as to find a piece of cellophane one evening, which David wrapped into a waterproof shield. The corners still felt so crisp, so official. The least he could do was tell Trixie he was leaving with a clean, dry document. Maybe he wouldn't even have to say the words. Maybe she would see it and accept it and forgive him. Maybe he could really just disappear. The leaves rustled and a nearby monkey cried out. Nobody's boots were that heavy. David tucked the papers away and fumbled for his pocket camera. He wiped the rain out of his eyes and tried not to breathe so hard. The footsteps were loud and wet and a steady rhythmic grunting echoed through the trees. No time for leaves or toucan dung. As the figure approached, it reached the chorus of "Jolene."

"I couldn't find you!" Trixie yelled. "I saw you leavin' and I thought you might get lost!" she struggled to cross a fallen branch, all wobbly in rubber boots that she once bought with Mama at the mall. She looked so helpless, so soft, her hair teased up and her eyes so wide. Her poncho draped her like a long gown. David's envelope felt heavy. Trixie finally jerked her foot up and over, turned back and kicked the branch for good measure. The envelope got a little bit lighter.

"I couldn't find you!" she yelled again, candy in her mouth, wrapper in the air.

"I was looking for you, too," David said.

"For what?" She looked so lost, so wet, mascara in little pools under her eyes. The answer was simple, but David decided it simply wasn't the time.

"Thought I saw a tropical mouse with something in its mouth. Thought it was an earring or something"

"My earring?"

"What?"

"The mouse, my earring?"

"No, or, I don't know, maybe." The envelope was practically on fire.

Trixie scrunched her face up and stared him down. David thought about confessing to the whole plan. If her makeup was already running, it would really be a kind gesture to save her the trouble. Mama never liked to waste makeup. Before David could talk himself into it, Trixie reached for something in her boot. She looked up, and squinted in the rain, a row of freckles showing under a layer of melted cover-up. So strange, so small. She put her hand out in a fist and opened it up. Two Tootsie Rolls.

"Well, I's just worried you wouldn't have enough."

One of the candies was partially unwrapped. David popped it into his mouth and nodded his way through another dose of required sweetness. Who cared if it was the right thing to do. It'd be a shame to just leave it there.

*

By the second week, David still hadn't gotten a grasp on the landscape. Nothing was nearly as charming. Everything was covered in mud—even the mud was covered in mud. The kissers got sloppier, the monkeys louder, the rainfall harder and harder. The Tootsie Rolls started sticking to David's insides. Trixie started to look off, her hair smaller and her face a little sloppier. Her voice more ragged when asking about the inheritance. She had lines that David had never even noticed before. She'd been busy, though. She'd somehow figured out how to spend money in a bartering system. Where others traded porn for smokes for food for sex, Trixie snooped around the grounds to find more makeshift toilet paper.

"Is this anybody's?" she'd say, holding up a loose leaf that blew in from the rain. The thieves would usually trade-off who answered.

"That's mine, Trixie," they'd say, before she even had the chance to hold it up.

"How much?"

"For you? $3.00." It was a steal. Literally.

"I just don't know how y'all make any money when you make so many exceptions," she said, pulling a soggy $5 bill out of the neckline of her poncho. "If we had a little more sunshine, I'd stay here forever."

It was good that she was open to moving. Maybe she wouldn't even ask for the house or the blender. Maybe she'd pack up and leave Freedom

Point and start a new life in Branson or Raleigh or Hollywood. They probably had condos there. Maybe she could sell the things on the Home Shopping Network. She could be so striking, so full of life like that. Whoever had her next would be mostly lucky. Mama'd love that. A tree branch broke somewhere off in the clearing.

"Hey," Trixie said in David's face, her arms wrapped tight, poncho-to-poncho. "Whatcha thinkin' bout?"

"Cheese club," David said. Trixie squeezed a little tighter.

"You don't fool me, I see you." Her hands rubbed his back under the plastic shield, her nails hitting the corners of the envelope. "I know what guilt looks like on you."

David nodded and shook his head all at once. It wasn't the time for clarity. He still had another week, at least. Maybe he could even wait it out a little longer. Trixie pulled him by his sleeve and led him back to their tent. She moved all hunched over, all slippery in the mud, and looked so awkward in way David had never seen. Older, weathered, worn down by the rain. He suddenly couldn't remember how Mama's gown had fit her at all. She took a seat on the dirt and pulled him down with her. The water was loud on the nylon. Trixie compensated.

"Listen," she said, a loud yelp. "I know things haven't been good since Mama died, God bless her soul, but I just want you to know that I know." She perched up on her knees and leaned in, her lips to his ear. Her voice dropped an octave or so. "I *know*," she said again, her voice lower than its usual chirp. White carnation cross was a million miles away. She scooted back and looked instantly sad. Of course she knew. Anybody who had any intuition would know, and Trixie had lots of intuition. She probably knew by Day 4 when she caught him rehearsing his exit speech with an old tree stump. She probably knew on Day 8 when he disappeared for the night or Day 10 when she caught him eating another woman's bread or Day 12 when he stopped rinsing off completely and just laid next to her like a pile of bones and mud and khaki scrap. She probably knew from the very beginning, and figured she could get one last free trip out of it. That's why she was so persistent, that's why she stopped trying to look like anything nice. It was so smart, so kind of her to start the conversation. She could be good like that sometimes.

"I know, all of it," Trixie said, "Everything. Better clean your act up and get back to business." She seemed a lot madder than what David imagined in his plan. It didn't look like she was going to forgive him for much.

Trixie let her threat hang in the air for a few seconds before she twisted her whole body around and pulled a cardboard box of candy out from under her pillow. Little scraps of sticks and leaves stuck out from the black and white Tootsie Roll wrappers.

"I know you been burying these," she said. She didn't even breathe as she waited for a response. That was all she had to say. It was so strange, so stunning. Trixie shook the box to make a point, the rattle of the inside mixing with the rattle of the rain. "You got anything to say?"

David tried to find a way to say that he had had enough, that he could barely feel his teeth, that the chocolate wasn't even really a bad habit, that he had been doing much worse, that Tootsie Rolls weren't really even chocolate, but some kind of terrible cousin of wallpaper paste. He tried to just say it already, all of it, but it all just seemed very mean. He would have to think of something nice to say to balance it out, a lot of nice things. Until then, he said the only thing he could think of.

"I must've dropped them, I can't believe it" in rigid monotone. He took the cleanest one out of the box and choked it down. All the sensation in his body stiffened up. It had been 16 days since he had a bowel movement that didn't feel like a candle was coming out. The piece went down in heavy chunk, like wet school eraser, so solid, so cold. Trixie rubbed his back and kissed him on the cheek. She was sweet like that, so warm, so kind. When she pulled away, she smiled a little.

"I knew Mama was wrong about you."

WHAT FELT LIKE A CENTURY OF DARKNESS SWEPT OVER CHERRAPUNJI as David struggled to stay on schedule. The yeti still hadn't surfaced, although two thieves told all of camp that they caught him and anybody who wanted to see him had to pay $10. It was easy to assume where the woman that used to be Trixie went that day. Who could really blame her, whoever she was, for believing, though. Belief in anything was a talent by the third week. David tried to believe that the plan still had a fighting chance that the rain might let up, that the candy might run out. He tried to believe that Mama might come to him in a dream, too, and tell him that he was a good boy no matter what he did. That wasn't the case. The rain never stopped, the trees all looked the same. The yeti never surfaced. Neither did Mama.

WHILE THE REST OF CAMP PLAYED CHARADES THAT NIGHT, THE McPhees snuck away to a clearing where David staged a going away party, dressed as a romantic dinner. Two logs served as dining chairs. He made a table out of loose branches and a nylon tent bag. Candlelight was a distant dream. David thought about waiting until they got back to Freedom Point, because maybe the candle was essential. Some thing that sort of resembled Trixie approached the party with an unwrapped pile of Tootsie Rolls on a makeshift aluminum tray. She held them up in the downpour, announcing their presence in a monologue for nobody.

"Here I come, eatin' only choc-o-late, all we eat, even though it's a baaad habit that we know NOBODY could help us break! Here we go, we gonna just sit here and eat them, my husband and me, here we are, look at us, nobody come out because we have to eat ALL this chocolate right here, right now." She wandered in a circle, her hair soaked into an uneven bob, her face all worn and featureless. David had to really look to see who she had become. She was the furthest from a carnation cross a woman could be. She was something else entirely, someone else that David didn't know at all. She kept up her circular wandering for so long that by the time the tray arrived at the table, all of the rolls had melted into one mutant pile of brown gloss. She smiled, whoever she was.

No more. It had to be tonight.

AFTER THE SECOND COURSE, TRIXIE-ISH STOPPED TALKING ABOUT THE deal she got on toilet paper, and what kind of curtains might look good in a condo once Mama's money finally came through, wherever it was, and started talking about David. She looked him in the eye and rubbed his hands, waxy film on her fingertips. Small eyes and dark teeth. It was such a strange mixture. He wondered how long she really was that way, and how she got away with it.

"I tell you," she said. "I know we had a rough year, what with Mama God bless her soul, but I'm glad that we can both just start over with a new beginn'n." Trixie shook her head and went on. "It's awk-a-ward, I know, to bring this up, but, I just can't watch you suffer no more with yourself."

The rain felt lighter. A tropical mouse chirped from the brush. Two sloths started mating in a nearby tree. Everything felt a little sweeter. Trixie went on.

"And I just been thinking about a lot of things—about you and me—and everything that's been going on here—and I want you to know that it's okay." She said it again, a little slower, softer. "It's okay, David. I forgive you, just have the decency to give it to me now."

She stopped there and let her head nod. The flashlight made her look so much softer or older or both. Of course she knew it was coming. She was smart like that, read people like that. It was so kind of her to simply save him from having to finally say it. Cherrapunji *was* a place of great relief.

David let the silence linger for a moment—all pure and sweet—before reaching for his back pocket. He stood a little, her eyes following, and pulled the cellophane envelope out. The flashlight made it look shinier, smoother. It felt almost invisible as David slid it across the makeshift table. Trixie shook her head, smiled a little. She looked surprised, but relieved. What a girl.

"I don'know why you thought you could hide this, but I forgive you," she said. "And whatever's in here, I'm sure it's more than enough." She touched his hair and reminded him what it was like to be loved. Adored, even.

"I hope so," David said. "You're so lovely."

"And I love *you*," she said. She picked up the envelope and held it up to her chest. She took a big breath, more than anybody needs, and, for the first time, whispered. "I knew Mama left me something."

An instant frost washed over David as it dawned on him that Trixie thought something else was coming, that some sort of reward or celebration was in store. He swore he heard thunder for the first time or a family of trees uproot and escape. Panic, loud and clear. Disaster. Maybe if he wished hard enough, some sort of fortune would actually be in the envelope and they could both just leave and enjoy eating solids again. Maybe the koala could come back, this time with a gun, and cut David a break and simply kill him, and Trixie could go on believing that she was worth fighting for, whoever she was. She was worth being covered in things that hint at I love you, and David wouldn't have to be another one to take that away. Maybe, just for once, it could be like Touch Soccer, like Gingerbread Club, and everybody could just join a team or build a home without getting hurt, no matter if it was right or wrong. He thought about diving across the brush branch table, across the wild space between them, and just saying it already—*I love you*— to see if it was really worth anything. He thought about doing a lot of things, but instead he just nodded.

The rest of the campers sang Kumbaya in the distance as Trixie peeled the cellophane off. She stopped a few times to wipe her eyes as the rain picked up and her poncho blew back. The trees rustled and a tropical mouse ran by. Trixie started talking about property values. She used her teeth to rip off through the last piece of the wrapper. A flock of birds abandoned a nearby eucalyptus. She put her thumb under the lip of the envelope and dragged it all the way across in a single tear. One of the flashlights blew away. Trixie tucked her whole body under the front of her poncho, and squinted to make out the paper details. David shined a flashlight on her to help her out, one last time. It stung to hear her voice trail off.

He winced as she started to get quiet, for what seemed like the very first time in their life together. Slowly, a vibrating ugly cry, almost unrecognizable. A long, drawn out silence and the muffle of her hands. Loud and wet and hard. When he finally opened his eyes, she was simply a balled up poncho. He watched her back breathe, up and down, slower and slower, and thought about Mama on the stoop in the same state.

Loneliness, loud and clear.

He let the flashlight fall and took his poncho off and put it on her shoulders. He stumbled around in the darkness and felt his way back to his side of the wilderness. The rain really fell for the very first time, all over his whole body, every part cold and fresh in a brand new way. A branch broke nearby as a fellow hunter finally interrupted. David shined the last remaining light on the ground to help them through the fallen brush. When he turned to see who it was, a mass of white fur emerged. Hands, feet, chest. Fresh fluff, practically glowing. Naked and blank. He stared at David and David stared at him, and they both wiped rainfall from their faces.

Neither of them had ever seen anybody so clean.

We Love You, Ben Bertram

BEN BERTRAM SURVIVED SLEEPAWAY CAMP, WHICH WAS A BLESSING AND a curse.

"It was crazy," he said, his parents looking grim with matching fudge sundaes in Freedom Point Diner. "They played the Electric Slide—the *Electric Slide*—and *nobody* else knew it but *me!* I mean no—"

"Ben," his mother said from across the booth. "Ben, it sounds like you had such a nice summer. It really does. And we are both so, so very proud that you finally had the chance to meet new friends and learn so, so many great things about Andrew Lloyd Webber."

She turned to Ben's dad who confirmed with the same noncommittal nod he'd been practicing ever since Ben asked to be both Laverne *and* Shirley for Halloween.

Ben's mom interrupted with a stretched out whine. "*...But...*" she said. "Before we drive home, we just want to tell you something. We want to tell you something, the sort of thing that may seem very terrible, the sort of thing that may place a damper on this homecoming celebration."

She raised her arms and showcased the dining room—the ketchup spill in the adjacent booth, the trail of salt leading to the restroom, the wallpaper border of sliced meat. A man came inside with a clip-on ponytail and ordered two frozen apple pies. Ben's mother took Ben's hands and ordered him to listen very closely.

"...*So* while this may be painful to hear," she said, "your father and I have to say this thing that we are about to say and we will try our hardest to be as directly gentle with you as we can be. Because we both decided that we are fully equipped to say this thing to you in a way we hope you will appreciate when you are much older and you aren't forced to keep in touch."

Ben squeezed his mom's hands and focused on her gaze, awaiting the announcement.

BEN BERTRAM RARELY TOOK THINGS WELL. EVEN AT BIRTH, BEN seemingly crawled out of the womb, rubbed his eyes, looked around, and tried to crawl back in. The same went for getting off the bus to go to school in thunderstorms, and attempting the annual rope climb in gym class, and other chancy activities that he deemed unspeakably terrifying. Around Fourth Grade, someone diagnosed Ben with acute anxiety, but things took a turn for the worst when Ben started to imagine bizarre scenarios that were rarely rooted in reality. In the Sixth Grade, Ben read on the Internet that ghosts are more likely to haunt children, because their souls are still fresh, which led to a less than favorable public meltdown when the lights went off at the school dance.

That's when the social conditioning began.

Mr. and Mrs. Bertram required Ben to join a few school clubs to keep himself busy, and ultimately, keep himself from himself, which was, initially, a great success. Ben found a few friends and won a ribbon in Junior Cheese Sculptors of America for a particularly thrilling Gouda showing. He passed out buttons at lunch during Wisconsin State History Month. He made a Pet Club collage about his cat, Muppet, and earned a spot in the Freedom Point Junior High library display case.

"Muppet and I keep each other safe," he wrote in permanent marker along the edge of the poster board. "We are just a couple of *old* souls."

Ben started to really loosen up by Eighth Grade. The panic attacks and the fetal crying seemed to almost slip away entirely, as Ben invested himself in more and more at school. He went on to serve as Recording Secretary for the Science Club, which was truly an art, according to Ben, before finding a real art with the Freedom Point Junior High Players, and, after years of inching further and further out of his comfort zone, Ben Bertram finally agreed to try summer sleepaway camp for one week.

Unfortunately, nobody knew what was about to be uncovered.

*

BEN'S MOM TRIED TO TREAD LIGHTLY ON HER SIDE OF THE DINER BOOTH, as to not spark some sort of long delayed meltdown.

"I'm going to say this thing now," she said, again, caressing Ben's hands. In a moment of weakness, she broke eye contact and let a disappointed whisper fall out of the corner of her mouth.

"*What comes first?*" she asked.

Without response, she whispered again.

"*What's first?*"

"I'm sorry," Ben whispered back, removing his hands and motioning to his chest, "but are you asking *me?*"

"NO," Ben's mother said, "give me back your hands, hold mine for reassuring comfort."

Ben placed his knuckles back into his mother's palms, his friendship bracelet from opening ceremonies resting under her thumb. She took a few deep breaths and began to silently mouth words, her eyes running over an invisible script on the ceiling. Unable to remember her next line, she began to whisper again.

"*Jerry,*" she said. Ben's dad snapped back from a long observation of passing traffic. "*What's first?*"

Ben's dad cleared his throat and replaced her hands, holding his son only by the fingers, as if unsure as to what they may be connected to. He held his breath before speaking.

"Son," he said. "Ben," he said. "We have to say this thing that we are about to say and we will try our hardest to be as direct with you as we—"

Ben's mom cut Ben's dad off, ripped their hands apart.

"That ship has sailed, Jerry." She made eyes at Ben and, again, lowered her voice to a whisper. "*What's after that?*"

"Like *I know.*" Ben's dad threw his hands up in a surrender. He reached into her purse and fished out a tiny a notebook full of things that Dr. Dennison had suggested.

"Finish your sundae," Ben's mom said with a threatening enthusiasm. Ben picked his spoon back up and shoved a layer of hard fudge in his mouth, per request. Ben's mom leaned into Ben's dad and the two began reading through clinical ideas for smooth conversation.

WHEN THEY FIRST STARTED SEEING DR. DENNISON, BEN'S PARENTS pretended to be confident in their abilities as bearers of bad news. By the second session, they had asked for direct quotations, for critical words, for succinct phrases that would make them sound worldly and wise, and, in turn, fit for comfort. Dr. Dennison did not oblige. He spoke in broad strokes of dated language, not far from that of a discount yogi. He encouraged free form spontaneous poetry in times of grief and he lectured in unclear metaphors seemingly ripped from a rough draft of *The Lion King.*

"My friends", he told Ben's parents once, "are my family and my family, my friends. And what one may call dark, I call brother."

"I think that is very interesting," Ben's mom said, Dr. Dennison nodding in agreement. "But we pick up our son from sleepaway camp in four days, and if you tell us exactly what to do, verbatim, I'm just saying— there will be an extra incentive, if you understand what I'm *saying*." Ben's mom played it cool, pulling on the collar of her denim blazer, winking at Dr. Dennison in a manner that resembled early signs of a stroke.

"Oh madam," Dr. Dennison said. "There is no perfect answer in a time of grief."

"$40," Ben's dad said, pulling out his wallet and tossing a thin piece of plastic on the table. "We'll give you $40 to Prime Cuts Steakhouse if you can wrap this up in twenty minutes."

THE POCKET NOTEBOOK SERVED AS THE ULTIMATE DIFFUSER FROM that point on. Ben's mom shifted her weight in the vinyl booth as she tried to read the notes.

"Ben," she recited, the script still in her husband's hands. "What would… what would you say…if? Okay yes, *if*, what would you say if I…*died*."

"YOU'RE DYING?" Ben screamed. Everyone in the dining room turned to look and somebody's ponytail fell off. Ben's mom matched his squeal, while Ben's dad sunk down into the vinyl.

"No!" she said. "No, I said just *imagine*, what would you say if I was—"

Ben's dad interrupted with a nudge, his eyes motioning to the notebook for her to reread. He used his pinky to underline a jagged cursive phrase, as Ben's mom followed along. She lifted her chin and began again.

"I'm sorry, *you're* dying, Ben."

"I'M DYING?"

"No no no, listen," she said. "If you were dying, what would *you* say to *me*?"

Ben shook his head side to side, his mouth wide open as he took a guess.

"I mean…I'd probably tell you that I didn't feel well, I suppose."

"Well, right" Ben's mom said. "We know that, because you're dying."

"Well then after that…after that…I guess I'd ask you to call my wife."

"Your *wife?*" Ben's dad asked. "Like…like a woman?"

Ben's mom slapped Ben's dad's chest and continued on with her own investigation.

"But what about right now, Ben, say you were dying now, and we all knew you were dying, and you had to say something to me—some sort of something beautiful—something comforting so that I could know that you were okay, what would you say? Like if, say, I wanted to remind myself…or others…that death is just a natural process that everyone endures."

Ben took his mother's hands and looked her in the eyes, his face scrunched up as he spoke from the heart. That was the nice thing about Ben's anxiety. He was always so honest—typically in hyperventilation— but, sometimes, not. As of late, he had a rational demeanor, though his ideas were still profoundly chilling.

"I would say," he said, "'Mom, just so you know, I'm going to die now and I'm disappointed that you let it come to this.'"

Ben returned to his sundae as his parents slowly eyed one another, re-strategizing their plan for attacking any kind of attack. The whole thing seemed to go a lot smoother during the rehearsals that Dr. Dennison recommended. A few times with each other and a few times in the mirror. Once with a propped up mop that slightly resembled Ben's curly mane. They had focused so hard on their end of the deal that they'd almost forgotten the possibility of a response.

In the booth, Ben's dad flipped through the notes and chose a section full of unclear arrows to work with. Mom began again.

"Okay, Ben, Ben—have... you... ever... thought... about... a... *sensh*..." She squinted and decoded in silence before Ben's dad helped her out.

"Seashell," he whispered.

"A SEASHELL," she said. "Have you ever thought about a seashell?"

Ben considered the question, his tongue across his lips and the plastic spoon still balanced in his hand. He tilted his head and seemingly fell deep into thought, his parents stunned by the effectiveness of such a stupid question. He winced a few times, before speaking.

"What *kind* of seashell?" he asked.

"What...*kind*?" his mom returned. "Like...what breed of seashell?"

"Well yeah," Ben said. "I mean, like, like a bivalve or a gastropod"

Ben's parents stared blankly across the booth.

Ben continued.

"Well...if I'm correct in my thinking, a bivalve is like, like what a clam lives in or..."

"...Or a mussel?" Ben's dad asked.

"Exactly," Ben said, pointing his plastic spoon with a great deal of enthusiasm.

"And a gastropod?" Ben's mom asked.

"Okay so a gastropod is like where snails live. Snails and hermit crabs, like, like things that go in and out...you know what I mean, like coil animals?"

Ben's parents nodded and spoke in overlapping verbal ticks, flipping frantically through Dr. Dennison's notes to locate specific follow-up questions for each sub-classification. Shockingly, Dr. Dennison only listed a single follow-up, which Ben's dad delivered with no commitment, one string of monotone recitation.

"Ben," he said, "Have you ever thought about how a seashell moves from place to place and by doing so it hears all the noises that we can only imagine."

"So you mean like a conch shell," Ben said.

"Sure," his father said. "Like a conch shell."

"Well, I guess I never thought of it that way. But—" Ben stopped mid-speech, the color from his face draining as his parents froze. A man dropped his tray at the register and Ben remained motionless, his parents enamored with what Dr. Dennison called the moment of calculation. Ben slowly regained movement, slowly bringing both hands to his cheeks. His fingers gathered at his nose and his eyes widened. His body began to shake as his breath spilled out in short bursts and his mom put her hands out, ready to catch his crumbling body.

Instead, Ben lit up.

"ARE WE GOING TO DISNEY?!"

Ben's parents looked to one another for an idea as to what was happening, Ben's speech spilling out all over the booth.

"Is that what you mean by the shell, the shell like the beach like Orlando like Disney like DISNEY WORLD? We're finally going to Disney World, aren't we?" All of his breath escaped his body. "We're going to Disney."

Ben's mom snatched Dr. Dennison's notes and whipped through each page, scanning the material for an emergency exit. *Shit,* she mumbled. *Shit shit shit* as Ben's dad lost all hope as Ben described the Fantasmic clips he'd watched on YouTube. Ben's mom tried to regain composure while her son vibrated across the table, her voice breaking in panicked revelations.

"Ben Ben Ben" she said "Ben Ben have you have you have you ever thought about *Heaven*? Ben have you Ben Ben have you Ben?"

Ben's father snapped and grabbed his son's hands, shouting across the sundaes.

"BEN, MUPPET DIED."

They all froze. Ben broke the silence.

"What?" he whispered, his hands still smashed between his dad's.

"Muppet died" Ben's dad said. "When you were at camp, Muppet died. She's dead. She died. Near the scratching post. We found her in the kitchen. We buried her in the garden. Beneath the swing, we put her there. We wanted you to know but didn't want to tell you."

Ben pulled his hands away from his father's and disappeared under the booth, his body balled up on the vinyl cushion, finding its way back into fetal comfort. He pulled the sleeves of his sweatshirt and let the arms hangs empty as he folded himself into the torso. The collar stretched as his face joined the darkness, his entire frame covered by the pilled cotton interior, a gentle shudder radiating its way up to the surface of his skin.

Ben began to whimper through heavy fabric.

Muppet he said *Muppet*   *Muppet*   *Muppet.*

Muppet in heaves of mixed mucus and dairy,

Muppet as his parents learned to listen from across the divide.

The Other Side

PART OF THE BOY DIES. THEN ANOTHER. THE REST OF HIM. BUT NOT before the boy learns some sort of lesson. He's alone when he learns the lesson, deep in the woods, in a bus. Nobody else is there when he learns it, not even his parents, not his friends, nobody. The boy is alone near some old home an animal once built. The boy is completely and utterly alone. That's why the lesson really counts. That's why he learns it for himself. It is all very sad and beautiful. This is what your teacher tells you.

She cries as you and your classmates look at words about the boy in desk copies from the library. You do it for three weeks and she cries every class. She cries and recites the words from the boy in the bus and you listen, but you don't really hear them. In fact, you don't really listen all the time either. You draw sunglasses on the photograph of the boy on the inside cover or imagine the girl from fourth hour P.E. doing the things you heard she may or may not do, depending on who you ask.

Your teacher carries on with her own private tragedy as you imagine what it might be like to hold that girl, to really be there face to face, alone, together, to have something to say that you've never said before. You imagine all of this when an Eighth Grade guy enters the classroom. He looks very cool but you don't let him know it. He holds a note. He gives it to your teacher. She reads it. She then gives it to you. You read it. You do not give it back. Instead, you exit the classroom and walk to the office. You take your things. You walk the long way so you don't look eager. You are eager, however. You feel panic. You move fast.

You reach the office door as instructed. You look through the window cut above the doorknob. You find your mother. She is a color you have never seen. You don't ask questions. You are not able to think of any.

When you exit the school, she tells you that she loves you and that *you are a becoming such a lovely young man.*

You ask if Grandma Bootsy died.

She tells you *no.* You are relieved but you are also indifferent. You feel guilty. Momentarily.

You ask your mother why she's still in her pajamas. Your mother begins to cry as you stand in the parking lot. You put your arms out, but you check for Eighth Grade guys first.

Your mother says *I tried; I tried* into your backpack strap. You really feel guilty, for many years. She holds you so close you swear your livers touch, your cheek on her flannel collar, her parka zipper loose on the side of your thigh. She tries to say something else as she holds you. When she can't, you should hold her, but you don't. You haven't learned that lesson yet. Instead, her phone rings and vibrates on your hip. She lets you go and pulls it out. She answers and pretends she was not crying. She says *no,* says *not yet,* says *we're leaving now.* You realize this is just the beginning.

When you reach the car door, your mother takes a deep breath. Then another. The passing period bell sounds as she looks for the keys to the car. You dance in place to keep warm and look busy as she takes her time and stops to blow her nose. She finds the keys and unlocks the car. You open your door as another bell sounds and class carries on without you. When you get in and buckle your seatbelt, you hear a noise from the backseat. You twist your body to find the source as your mother starts the car. You find it. You see it. You panic. You move in reverse as your mother exits the lot. No one says a word.

On the drive, your mother tries to pretend that things are not falling apart. She asks if you really like junior high, if it's true that the rich kids still get ice cream at Freedom Point Diner after school. She tells you that the girls seem very cute. She asks if the Grade Sevens and Eights are nice. She doesn't address the howl from the backseat. It's louder, almost lonesome. It gets sadder. It feels deeper.

Between howls, there is a silence in the car. Your mother asks you if you're ready for what might happen. Whatever you do, say yes. Even if you don't mean it. Nobody ever does.

When you reach your destination, your dad is there with his new girlfriend. Your mother parks and lines your window up with his and you wave to one another. His girlfriend waves a beat behind you both. Your mother doesn't wave at all. She turns the car off and you all exit. Your father tells his girlfriend *maybe another time* and she gets back in the car and locks the doors. She looks around the inside of purse because there isn't anything else to do.

She does this while your father removes his coat. He rolls his sleeves and takes his watch off. He asks you to hold both. You put your arms out and feel small beneath the pile. It feels heavier than you expected. Your father opens the car door and leans into the backseat. He disappears for a long time. Your mother continues to cry. He surfaces with a heap in his arms. It's wrapped up in an orange towel. The howl is at its loudest. Your father yells over the noise and asks if you want to trade. He tells you *this is it*. He tells you *take her in*. He tells you *she would want it this way*. Your mother takes your father's things; your arms are free to take the heap. You kick the salt on the pavement, play with the earring you heard might be cool, say *I can't*. He says *take her*, you say *I can't*. He says *be a man for me* and you choose not to. You shake your head *no*, snowfall collecting in your hair. You chicken out. You are not the hero.

Your father leaves. He runs and your mother follows with all of his things in her arms. His girlfriend watches from behind her car window. Your father runs and the heap goes with him. It bounces all around, whiskers everywhere, the orange towel smaller and smaller as they cross the lot. You follow because you have to. You follow and when you reach the door, the cold comes with you. A poodle in a cone looks mad near the waiting area. Everybody else has got your teacher's look in their eyes—especially the girl behind the desk. She tells you *second room*. She makes her face look extra sad for you. You look to your dad and your mom and the heap, and you wish you were back with that P.E. girl. Your mother and father lead. You follow.

The doctor tells you terrible things about the heap, but he says them so fast that you don't have time to feel terrible. Then he says nice things about you. He tells you that you are such a lovely young man. He calls you by the wrong name. He tells you to say a final prayer *if that sort of thing interests you* and your mother starts talking to Baby Jesus. *Baby Jesus*, she says, *Baby Jesus I'm not ready. I'm not ready,* louder, *I'm not ready,* and your father makes ocean noises in her ear to calm her down. The howling tapers off until it stops. The room falls silent. Everyone panics, but nobody shows it. The doctor runs his hand over the heap on the table. He asks if you want to keep the towel.

Your mother asks for a moment and the doctor leaves the room.

She asks again until you and your father leave too. Your father for good. When the door shuts, you hear your mother in little spills.

She says *you are my best friend.*

She says *they don't know what we've seen.*

She says *thank you for always being on my side.*

You hear her sing "Rainbow Connection."

There isn't anything else to hear.

Your mother opens the door and asks if you have anything to say. You don't, but you pretend to. You trade places and step into the room with your eyes closed. She shuts the door and leaves you on the other side.

You are alone. You are frozen wet in a room of matching whites. When you open your eyes, you understand that this is it. The heap looks even smaller on the table. It doesn't look like it expects much of you, but still, you try. You try for your mom. For your dad. For the P.E. girl. You pick up the heap without the towel and hold it close and slow dance. You close your eyes and feel its heat, its matted fur on empty bone, and move your feet without a plan. The Eighth Grade guy doesn't deliver any more directions and Baby Jesus is busy. You hold the heap and say *I'm here.* You are alone when it counts most.

It Was

RIGHT BEFORE THE CREDITS, IT WAS CRISP, CLEAR EXHALE.

It was alone but not lonely, long awaited let go.

It was hospital orderly in utility blues and late night goodbye hush hush.

Go on, Joanna. It was a pleasure seeing you.

Right before the very end, it was whole milk pudding and life wires, and some wet cough from the patient next door.

There was invisible music, too, in the end, some old violin or string sort of something, some kind of sunset ballad or horse gallop, but before that, for what seemed like centuries, before mind and body made a pact to work together—before alone but not lonely—it was

TEN YEARS OF CHARLIE AND HIS MANNEQUIN COLLECTION. IT WAS middle-aged pastel strip mall sweethearts and backroom overtime restock kissing and a knock-off ring from the jewelry department. There was no music, just motion. Charlie living to dress and undress, piece-by-piece, sock by sock. It was head to toe inspection and *let's play a game where you are still like a body.* It was trying so hard not to breathe during sex, then during sleep, then during daylight, where Charlie made manager and took stock home. Old boots. Suede hats. Giant chest full of something heavy. It was *don't come in the basement unless you're invited* and Crystal at the top of the top stair spying and Charlie underneath the weight of women's limbs and plastic waistlines. They were all so slim and young and hungry, like Crystal, when she was "Luster," and lived to please

SHERRIFF SUGAR DADDY. NO TALK. ALL HANDS. EXTRA MONEY IF she'd lose her top, extra if she'd bring buffalo wings into the Champagne Room. Even more if she called herself a piece of rotting garbage slut from time to time. It was mouth to mouth martini breath and an olive back and forth for effect and Christmas bonus to fix those boobs and gain some weight and have some meat. It was alley jerk off thank you card near a dumpster full of spoiled Bailey's. It was all tongue and dirty teeth and Crystal in abbreviated whispers. *Ask me what I want even though I'm trash. Ask me anything and I'll tell you something good.* It was always lingering silence and voiceless zipper dropped and deep throat spit swap cupped balls finish and end of night wet nap and long drive back home to

ANDREW FROM CRAIGSLIST AND HIS ANNOTATED BIBLE. IT WAS DRY sandpaper kissing lessons for a free sleeping bag on the floor. It was warm Sprite from the can and over the clothes touch therapy, so that Andrew could forget about Gabriel from the ranch. Satan's test and God's call and friends helping friends from becoming themselves. It was rare evening of not enough touch and Crystal stripping down piece by piece and Andrew in a panic gasp.

I'm saving that for somebody real.

It was lingering silence and consolation handshake and sickeningly sweet soda break, the air all candied like

VICTOR BACK IN HIGH SCHOOL, BEFORE COLLEGE DORM ROOM BREAKUP over microwave spaghetti, before Crystal made a living off shrinking into a fantasy. High School Victor and Sometimes Crystal, before Charlie, Daddy, Andrew and his Bible. Before final sunset escape, alone but not lonely, Victor Back In High School, always soaked in fast food soda, drifting by like a tumbleweed, until prom night hair gel cleanse and burgundy rental tux and private backseat party in the Freedom Point Rentals parking lot. High School Victor in steady hump and forced mustache all sharp and moist, noisy climax, and acne glow. Crystal ripped in two and tiny blood spot south of a bobby pin scalp poke. It was only terrible for a little bit, the stretching of the thinnest parts. It was mostly only right after how much he spent on tickets. Victor like some rogue cattle that enrolled in boyhood, bulky and glazed, something sticky. Loud huff and heavy pant. *Make more noise so I can get hard again. Stick them out so they look bigger.* Victor in heat. Crystal in rebound, secretly waiting for some last gesture from

GEORGE PEABODY AND HIS DIRTY DENIM VEST AND HIS STUPID HAIRCUT and his lousy arrowhead collection that almost nobody ever talked about because it was SO embarrassing, but it was his, and she was too, once. George Peabody in Freshman Gym and silly class do-si-do, dancer naming, partner bow. Freestyle choice. George and Crystal. Careful hug in chance slow dance, like everything might be okay to believe in. Crystal in quick peck full of fire stuff and girl squeals and glitter dust and wanting to be wanted so badly. It was George Peabody erection interruption. Shades of red and anxious stumble and *cool it, okay* while he walked it off. It was cool for another two years in like-like, in classroom low-key smile and after school kind of movie thing. Root beer float, separate straws. It was something like chivalry or honor or kindness, something good and mostly enjoyable. Two blocks to his back door, fifteen stairs up to his room, two knocks to enter, Nicholas Cage in something or other, back home by streetlights. New day, same routine. Two blocks fifteen stairs up to his room, two knocks Nicholas Cage. Two blocks, stairs, knocks, and some cross-town lonely weirdo girl, her hands all over a root beer float—one straw. It was whiplash and loose puzzle pieces and sudden sort of blubber feeling. George Peabody in shades of red, hand in hand with some new somebody, Nicholas Cage sniper explosion, George in *wait hold on*, in *please don't cry*, in *Karlee hates when people cry*. Eight stairs out and two block sprint. Lengthy sobbing milkshake coma. Lots of straws.

THAT'S HOW IT ENDED, THE FIRST TIME, BEFORE SWEATY HUMP Heavenly Savior Back Alley Blowjob Plastic Boobs and the final thrill of being left alone, fully and completely. George Peabody was the first to leave, but by no means was he the first. Before the final sunset, before Charlie, before Sherriff before Andrew Victor George and the ones that didn't make a mark in time, there was

BODY HEAT AND BALLOON POP AND EDIBLE GOLD AND MIDNIGHT CACKLE background loop. It was only the most meaningful Freedom Point Junior High students and Tally Majors' Hollywood Birthday Bash. It was sensory overload, loose rules and tight handholding, and Tally's mom's sort of boyfriend on sort of supervision. It was curse word rap, unedited. Burnt out glow sticks all over the floor and hollowed out girls on Tally's new crash diet.

*

TALLY TOLD THE GIRLS THAT THEY ALL LOOKED GOOD AND ALL THE boys tried to accidentally feel a boob on purpose during surprise tickle torture attacks. Tally's mom's sort of boyfriend supervision resignation, quick trip back upstairs. *No rules, hell yeah* high-five chorus. Somebody's idea to play Seven Minutes in Heaven, and a line that disappeared into a closet, two by two. Crystal especially hungry for something, maybe even Tommy DiMicci behind his plastic cup. No ice. So hot. Couples went in and out of the closet, resurfacing in matching lip gloss and back rub, until all that remained was Crystal and Tommy.

Slow motion realization.

Sudden anxiety.

Heavy heartbeat.

Dumb joke from Jacob Kentor about making a baby or something, and basement door interruption, and Tally's mom's sort of boyfriend in an announcement meant for Crystal. Cordless phone in the air, mom and dad on the other end. Whole group whine about kissing cop out and Crystal in secret sigh of relief. Out the basement door, up the stairs, in the kitchen, phone back on the hook. Awkward linger parade.

TALLY'S MOM'S SORT-OF BOYFRIEND WATCHED SOME OLD WESTERN about a girl trapped on a train track and cleared a spot on the couch. *Come on over* wave. *False alarm, wrong number, but stay a little.* Some sort of rampage downstairs, and cool quiet on the main floor. Soft couch. Extra pillows. Tally's mom up in bed and her sort of boyfriend officially renamed Todd. Todd in funny joke about his own fourteenth birthday, about how dumb teachers are and something called the hustle. Crystal in spaghetti straps and liquid eyeliner and calorie counting. Sort of grownup. Todd in *you look pretty if you don't know that at your age.*

Todd in soft back massage and western girl tied up at the wrists. Noisy whistle from downstairs and quiet hand on Crystal's neck. Todd in little seat shift sigh and head tilt forward and lip-to-lip. Train headed straight for western girl. Crystal in nervous sit still breath and Todd's tongue in freeze tag poke. Stomach drop and inside guilt and neck jerk and *sh sh sh*. Todd in eye contact serious whisper.

YOU DON'T HAVE TO LIKE IT FOR IT TO BE GOOD

IN AND OUT, LIP GLOSS SWAP, ROUGH SCRATCH FACE HAIR JAW MASSAGE and sort of secret inside flutter. Risky spaghetti strap drop.

Upstairs bedroom toilet flush.

Todd in sudden stop and turn away and antsy angry anti-contact. Silence as a train passed through. Todd in *cover yourself up, nobody wants to see that*. Spaghetti strap replacement and instant loss of appetite. Slow rise and silent exit.

A WAVE OF STEAM FROM THE BASEMENT DOOR, HOTTER ON THE WAY down, hotter from the inside out, bulky thighs and belly fat, seemingly surfacing from nowhere. Brand new longing tension shame. Suck it up and suck it in. Everybody in truth or dare and kid stuff and couch snuggle. No pillows. Somebody pecked somebody and everybody screamed.

It was Crystal's turn eventually.

It was play along, but feel alone.

It was pick a crush, anyone.

It was so loud, it was hard to breathe.

Inventory

CHEETO DUST IN THE MORNING, FIRST THING, FIRST THOUGHT.

Cheeto dust for breakfast, Cheeto dust for pre-breakfast, Cheeto dust before toothbrush; Brush light. Toothpaste counts as calories.

Breakfast after Cheeto dust, bright orange first, lay the foundation.

Breakfast only if breakfast is served.

Stomach rumble is Cheeto dust settling, reward yourself with chewing gum.

Blow a bubble, live it up.

Let yourself enjoy yourself, hollowed out, Cheeto dust, maybe breakfast, maybe not.

NOTHING WITH A CRUST FOR LUNCH, NOTHING THAT LEAVES CRUMBS. Try a diet soda, try it with a straw, try a Gatorade, try a new flavor, let yourself enjoy yourself.

Pretend it's an island drink and you are in a bikini.

Remember the bikini, remember the mall and remember the mirror and remember the bikini and sip slowly and enjoy. The burn is just the Cheeto dust mixing, the heavy bright orange paste inside. Think about that. Still want a bagel?

Who needs a bagel when you can have a bikini, who needs a bagel when you can have a boyfriend, plenty of boys like younger girls, boys that drive and touch below the waist, boys, a whole bunch of them, waiting for you to be your best. Let them have a taste, look good, forget the bagel, take a sip and seem sweet and look good in case they drive by the bus stop, look soft, look fragile, wait it out until the ride comes. Get on board and go to the back and treat yourself with a snack.

Think about what you deserve and let yourself have what you think everyone else is having.

A banana is a gift; a box of raisins won't stick.

Anything with crusts or crumbs comes later when the enemies are watching.

Don't let the enemies serve you, serve yourself, and push the food around.

Two bites every three to five minutes, each bite half a fork.

If the enemies ask you questions, take a break and answer, and let them shave a few bites off.

How many bites did you have? Was it worth it? Feel it pile on your insides? Feel it settle on top of the Cheeto dust, the orange paste, the saliva stuff, the processed goop?

Now do you still want dessert?

Go ahead and take dessert, let yourself go before inventory. Chew slow and treat yourself, you did good and the boys know it. You did good, but you could've done better. Don't you think you could've done better?

You'll have to wait and see when it settles, when the moon comes out and the enemies go to bed. When the enemies go to bed, go to the bathroom and use your toothbrush.

Make sure it's clean. Toothpaste counts as calories.

USE THE BRISTLE SIDE AND IF YOU CHOKE, YOU'RE DOING RIGHT.

Stop for air, you deserve it.

STOP FOR AIR, BUT DON'T STOP FOR GOOD, LET IT ALL COME BACK UP and out and into the toilet, let the tile on the floor cool you off when it gets hard.

Try to keep quiet, try not to wake the enemies, try to stay calm.

Think of the beach and the bikini and the boyfriend counting on you. Let your insides all fall out, every little bit counts, every little choice you made in a moment of weakness. Think about the new life and try a little harder.

When your finished, checked the bowl, check the texture, check the color.

If it's clear-clear syrup, you've only just begun.

Look for dust, Cheeto dust, bright orange stringy stuff.

Look for the first choice you made in the pit of your stomach.

Look for the beginning of it all, and be proud.

Be proud and feel happy, but don't think it's over.

Everyone is counting on you.

Do you still want dessert?

Headliners

IN THE END, RAT TAIL WORE A NECK BRACE.

Before that, an ACE bandage, wrapped around some loose flesh that dangled from where his chin used to be. People gasped, people cringed. A Booster Mom brought an athletic towel courtside to Coach Henry, who pretended to know how to reduce the pain.

The Dance Squad sat Indian style across the floor and formed two prayer circles—one for Rat Tail and one for their testy Mariah Carey stereo track. The opposing team feigned sympathy by crowding around and looking disgusted.

"Oh man," they said. "Are you crying?" they said. "Oh man," they said.

Coach shielded Rat Tail's face on the court, his khakis covered in sneaker dust and streaky blood, as an ambulance pulled up to Freedom Point Junior High.

Two first-year EMTs kicked a basketball out of the way as they pushed a stretcher into the gym. They took photos with their phones of Rat Tail's mangled chin flesh and asked him if he was, in fact, crying. They wheeled him out on a stretcher and Coach followed. The whole gym applauded.

RAT TAIL DIDN'T ALWAYS WANT TO BE THE MASCOT.

He made it abundantly clear on the bathroom wall that the Freedom Point Settler was, in fact, a fag.

"Constitution, freedom of speech," he later said, his leg draped over a conference chair in Coach's classroom. "Wouldn't have said it if it wasn't true."

Coach Henry rolled his sleeves and reclined at his desk, his body disappearing in an oversized dress shirt. He cleared his throat and made eye contact with two girls who ran for the bus in the hallway. He stared at a map of Switzerland on the ceiling, then a string of globes that lined the back of the classroom. That's all the time he could waste before he had to say something, anything.

"How does it make you feel?" he said.

"That the Settler is a fag? Lousy I guess. Bitch looks like a broke-ass dandy."

Coach took to his feet and closed the classroom door, while Rat Tail cracked his neck and walked around the room. His headphones played background hip-hop from the front of his pelvis. A giant Walkman was tucked between the waistband of his jeans and a baggy t-shirt that said

"Big Money" in magic marker on the chest. Rat Tail dragged his feet around the room and stopped in the back corner below a laminated map.

"My uncle owns an island," he said. He lifted his arm like a zombie and pointed at the print. "That one."

"Your uncle owns Hawaii?"

"Yup," Rat Tail said, crossing back in a slow swagger. "Have you heard of it?"

Coach rubbed his eyes with his fingertips.

"I guess what I want to know is why you signed your name."

"Where?" Rat Tail asked.

"On the bathroom wall."

"Why?" Rat Tail asked.

Coach Henry snorted and put his palms up in surrender.

"Well how do you know I did it? You know it's illegal to judge me by the color of my skin." Rat Tail crossed his arms, both of which were white.

"I know you did it," Coach said, "I saw your name. Why'd you think I asked you to stay after?"

"Shit, I don't know," Rat Tail said. "Figured you saw me cheat on yesterday's quiz." Rat Tail laughed to an invisible audience as Coach sat back down in his desk chair. He let out a long overdue sigh.

"Well let's agree to pick our battles," he said. "Off to practice."

"Yeah, okay," Rat Tail said. "I can stick around for that."

Coach stood up and pretended to know what was happening. He pocketed a whistle from his desk and stretched his words out.

"Right…well no…need to," he said. "The team's…probably got it… you know…covered, so…" He bent his knees and leaned back and pursed his lips.

"Don't matter," Rat Tail said. "Gary don't pick me up until 5:00 anyways, so. Sometimes 5:30 because Gary got burned real bad by a Bloomin' Onion so now he gotta wrap his hand every night after his shift."

"And Gary is…"

"My new step dad," Rat Tail said. "He works at Prime Cuts, the one near Firecracker Casino. He smells like mayonnaise, but he lets me drink beer, so." Rat Tail put his fist out for an unreturned bump as Coach motioned to the door. They walked together.

The trip to the gym took twice as long because Rat Tail had to limp because an music video said it was in. Then he had to call two girls hanging posters "fine ass bitches."

"It's a good thing you asked me to stay today," Rat Tail said. "Usually I'm booked up."

Coach had heard about Rat Tail's daily activities through his infamous disciplinary reports: One count making weapons out of mechanical pencils. One count writing rap lyrics on the bathroom wall. One count smelling Sharpies. One count with no pants near the National Geographics. One count smoking during the Blizzard Blast. One count attempted arson. One count eating sawdust off the janitor's cart.

"What do you usually do?" Coach asked.

"Study," Rat Tail said. "I don't know, what do you usually do?"

Coach thought about his own activities: One count taking a nap. One count asking mom if the mail came. One count unpacking a box. One count Googling Catherine's new boyfriend. One count Googling himself. He wondered if the new guy could take initiative like she wanted. One count Googling "initiative" just to be sure of what she meant. One time, Coach bought a wine cooler and watched a show about Barbados with his mom's Lhasa Apso. Then he bought a bathing suit on a clearance website. Catherine got engaged. The bathing suit was non-refundable.

"What do I do?" Coach asked. "I grade."

Rat Tail shook his head. "Shit's bad for you man. You know Malcolm 10?"

"Malcolm X, yes," Coach said.

"Yeah yeah," Rat Tail said. "You know, he died from reading too much computer screen?"

"You don't say."

Rat Tail raised his voice as they entered the gym.

"Yeah," he said. "Gary told me that. Heard about it from some blackjack dealer. He knows some fucked up shit."

Coach nodded along and watched the mighty-mighty Freedom Point Settlers in action. A dozen air balls bounced off the walls. Two boys picked scabs at center court. Assistant Coach Drews played Tetris on a phone and sat off to the side and out of the way. Rat Tail seemed to enjoy each time that somebody missed a basket. Coach wondered if they'd ever win a game, how much initiative was required, how many games it would take to get in the newspaper like the other junior high teams. He wondered if Catherine got the newspaper, if she ever looked for him in there.

"These guys are bitches," Rat Tail said. He clapped for another air ball.

"Do you play?" Coach asked.

"Shit yes I do, spider-dribble is my bitch."

"Point taken," Coach said. "I bet you could school me."

Rat Tail put his hand on Coach's shoulder and looked real serious.

"Bitch, why you gotta bring yourself down, man."

"I'll work on it," Coach said, fishing for the whistle in his pocket. He put the metal in his mouth and blew three times, then once more to mean business. Then twice more. The team rounded up and Coach told them what they ought to be doing. When that seemed too complicated, he asked them to simply run the halls. Two kids swore they had sprained ankles. One pointed to his wrist. The rest took off in a mad dash towards the vending machines.

Assistant Coach Drews announced that he finished Level 7.

Coach Henry took a seat on the edge of the bleachers and watched two of the injured players horse around. He wondered if they could get in the newspaper if they came in second, or even if they won some kind of sportsmanship award. Maybe one of the players really *was* injured— so badly that it could be considered a handicap. People would love to read about the Coach who put the handicap kid on the court at the last second. Catherine would love something like that. Catherine loved seeing people suffer.

Rat Tail called the injured players *bitches* under his breath and took a seat next to Coach. He mumbled with a stone cold face.

"Those bitches are lying, they isn't injured," he said. Coach cut him off.

"Language," he said.

"Fuck that shit," Rat Tail said. "Freedom of speech."

"Point taken." Coach put his hands up in surrender as Rat Tail kept going.

"And FBI..."

"FYI..."

"Yeah, FYI," he said, "I got Ms. Jarvis for English, and she's old as shit, so maybe she wrote the language and *I'm* the right one."

Coach laughed and nodded—his whistle, too, in a rhythmic jingle.

"I won't fight you on that one," he said. "Do you know how old I am?"

"61," Rat Tail said.

"Close. I'm 34. You know what that means? Mrs. Jarvis is literally 30 years older than me. Mrs. Jarvis has almost lived two of my lifetimes."

Rat Tail laughed without reservation, a goofy rasp that made his whole body shake like a little baby.

"Bitch, you oughtta do standup," he said. "You do standup?"

"No," Coach said. He shook his head and laughed a little. "Just Geography."

"S'okay, bitch. You still got another lifetime."

Coach smiled at Rat Tail and put his hand out. The fist bump was returned.

Three members of the basketball team walked by the gym doors eating chips. They made eye contact with Rat Tail and walked a little quicker out of sight. Coach asked Rat Tail why he never tried out for the team. "I talked up try outs at least twice a week in class," he said.

"I don't really listen in class."

"Alright," Coach said. "But your uncle owns Hawaii, so, at the very least, I know you know how to *travel* with a ball."

"Bitch, I don't know," Rat Tail said. He chewed on the sleeve of his t-shirt and then picked at a cuticle. "I don't like the drama of it," he said. "I don't like the drama of team sports and I wanna call the shots."

"What drama?"

Across the gym, the injured started slapping each other again. They threw elbows until Coach blew his whistle. Twice.

"Bitches," Rat Tail whispered, shaking his head.

"Totally," Coach whispered back. "You know," he said. "We need a new mascot." Coach tapped his feet and spoke real slow. "Ben had to take a personal leave, you know—pet death, you know how it goes." He spoke even slower, a long stretch again. "You wouldn't...happen to know anyone...would you?"

Rat Tail shook it off and adjusted the Walkman on his waistband. He leaned his weight back and forth until his eyes went wide in a wash of realization. He cocked his head to the side.

"Bitch, please."

"You get a Gatorade every game and all you have to do is walk around."

"Bitch, please."

"I won't let you drink beer, but I don't smell like mayonnaise."

Rat Tail laughed.

"You get a whip."

"What kind?"

"Retired jump rope or something," Coach said. "Every settler needs a whip. Especially the ones that aren't allowed to have guns or knives or hatchets."

Rat Tail rolled his eyes and shook his head.

"Okay, " Coach said. He almost stopped right there, but he just couldn't help it. "You know we might be in the newspaper this season."

Rat Tail lit up and turned his volume down.

"For what?"

"I don't know, maybe if we win a game or something. Maybe just for trying. You ever been in the newspaper?"

"No. But Gary's in the newspaper a lot because he does stuff without thinking about it first." Coach nodded and pretended to know what that could possibly entail. Rat Tail turned the Hip Hop all the way down.

"You know," he said. "Maybe I could be in the same newspaper as Gary. Like we could be in it together, the same exact one, both of us. Together. Bitch, that would be cool, huh?" Rat Tail smiled in a way that Coach had never seen before. He looked instantly younger, or maybe just his own age for once, and Coach played a part in that. He played a big part, like a mentor or something. A mentor for a kid that didn't seem to have much else going on. *That* should be in the newspaper. *That's* initiative.

"You know," Coach said, "I bet the newspaper could put you and Gary on the same page."

"Fuck yeah," Rat Tail said. "I bet they could." Coach watched Rat Tail get lost in a dream as the team started trickling back into the gym. Kids laid out on the court and complained about leg cramps and Rat Tail turned back to Coach.

"Get me my weapon."

THE WHIP DIDN'T LAST VERY LONG. MOST OF THE COSTUME DIDN'T. During his first practice, Rat Tail got the tip of the old jump rope stuck in a coin slot while trying to snake his way into a vending machine. Another time, he brought his wide-brim hat home to show Gary, but when it returned, somebody had ripped the whole top off and patched it up with duct tape, a sloppy *Sorry* written in magic marker across job. Coach let Rat Tail add a big gold chain to the costume after Rat Tail promised to mention him if the newspaper ever called his house. Rat Tail let Coach try the necklace on when he promised to stop being such a little bitch all the time. When Coach put it on, Rat Tail laughed and Coach had Assistant Coach Drews take a picture of the two of them on his phone. Rat Tail asked Coach to send it to the newspaper because Gary had a story coming up.

"He sold all his teeth on the internet," he said. "Did you know that's illegal?"

Coach wondered what kind of nice thing Catherine might say once she saw it, the story about Rat Tail and about himself. He wondered if the bathing suit might get some use after all. When he sent the picture in, he included a list of suggested headlines: "Student & Mentor Find School Pride." "Unlikely Boy Finds Place In The World."

Nobody from the newspaper ever wrote back.

WHEN RAT TAIL'S FIRST GAME ROLLED AROUND, HE SAT OUT BECAUSE somebody moved his Walkman and justice is justice, motherfuckers. He still got the Gatorade because, for the first time, he stopped calling Alaska a planet, and the following week, he took to the court in what was left of his ensemble: an old flannel button down and a pair of burlap pants. A single suspender. A white paper beard. A long line of tied up jump ropes and a makeshift walnut cracker handle. A gold plastic chain with a dollar sign pendant and a new pair of sneakers that Coach bought him.

They took another photo for the newspaper when he tried them on.

"When is Gary and me gonna be in it?" Rat Tail asked.

"I don't know yet," Coach said. "They still have to figure some things out." Coach sent about two dozen emails without any response. He even changed the subject lines every so often: "Coach & Mascot Tackle Adversity." "Coach Gives Mascot Gift Out Of General Goodness." "Coach Takes Initiative In Freedom Point."

The crowd always cheered when Rat Tail walked the perimeter of the gym every 15 minutes, just like Coach said they would. Coach gave Rat Tail a fist bump every time he passed the bench. One game, a Booster Mom let Rat Tail choose two Gatorades because he walked every 10 minutes because "freedom of speech." Another time, Rat Tail did a moonwalk that he learned from the Dance Team girl who wore the shortest skirt. Even the other team cheered. That's when Coach let Rat Tail line up and shake hands with the other players at the end. Luckily, only four of them were bitches.

"Take my picture!" Rat Tail said. "Tell the newspaper!" After game 5, Coach told Rat Tail he was real proud of him, even if the newspaper was taking a long time. Rat Tail responded by telling Coach about the Wyoming state bird.

HALFWAY THROUGH THE SEASON, RAT TAIL WAS LATE TO A GAME AFTER eating Taco Bell two towns over with some of the players after school. They said he simply vanished, had even ditched a bag of loose change and cinnamon twists. It wasn't hard to imagine the headline: "Man Loses Child Because He Didn't Take Initiative." Coach called Rat Tail's directory number at the start of the game and left a voicemail. Then he called again and said the same things, but louder, maybe even slower, if possible. By halftime, a warped Mariah Carey sang backup on the third voicemail. On the court, Coach told the team to pay attention to the game, that they can't just do whatever they want because rules are there for a reason because otherwise people just get let down because the newspaper might show up and it isn't fair to leave them hanging.

Assistant Coach Drews told everybody that he finished Level 49.

The players went back out on the court as the Dance Team hugged each other after another strong showing. The side doors to the gym opened. Rat Tail stepped inside. He took a hunting vest off and began rubber-banding a beard from his back pocket onto his face. A Booster Mom approached with a cold bottle and the game picked up. Coach watched Rat Tail stall before assuming his usual path. The gym doors opened again and a man in his mid-twenties entered. He carried in an old jump rope whip while the cheerleaders started Battle Cry. The man wore a bigger vest that matched Rat Tail's, and his right hand was wrapped up in napkins and mailing tape. Rat Tail handed him his vest and took the whip, all giddy and lit up. He untangled a knot near the end and started his journey across the floor while the man pulled a phone from his back pocket.

Two fouls were called in the time it took Rat Tail to round a quarter of the court. Coach watched the man with the mailing tape hand text on his phone without looking up. Then Coach watched Rat Tail take two steps before striking the ground with the jump ropes and looking back towards the man. Rat Tail waved. The man texted. Rat Tail took another slow step and looked back, and the process repeated itself. Coach watched for a solid 15 minutes as Rat Tail tried to keep his beard on and walk tall. When he finally made it half way, he briefly looked to Coach, who repeated his halftime pep talk while Rat Tail cleared his nose.

"What if the newspaper came?" Coach said. Rat Tail's voice cracked.

"He needed help with his hand," he said.

"I don't care, Rat Tail. Is that Gary?"

"I don't want to talk about it," Rat Tail said.

"What if I needed you for something?"

"I don't want to talk about it."

Rat Tail continued on and they didn't cross paths for the rest of the game. At the last buzzer, the team celebrated their single-digit loss as Rat Tail filed out of the gym in a hurry, his whip dragging as he straightened his beard and picked something out of his eye. The man with mail hand followed close behind, occasionally stepping on the whip and yanking Rat Tail backwards. Before leaving, he stopped and waved his damaged hand at Coach, who made a point to look busy. When Coach got home, he went through the newspaper one last time to make sure he didn't miss his headline. On the bottom of page six, the newspaper printed a picture of Catherine and her new husband in honeymoon bathing suits. Some island, somewhere.

The next day after class, Rat Tail apologized.

"It wasn't Hawaii," he said.

He said it so soft that Coach barely heard it.

"It wasn't Hawaii. My uncle doesn't own Hawaii."

"That's okay," Coach said. "I don't think anyone really does."

*

THE SEASON CAME AND WENT, BUT THE HEADLINE NEVER DID. AT THE end of the very last game, Rat Tail got too wild off of three Gatorades and started yelling "pussy" at no one in particular. When Coach asked him to take a break, he watched the game from behind one of the hoops and clapped his hands for everything but the air balls. Coach looked for Gary in the stands, but didn't see anyone with irregular hands. He was probably out with Catherine, ruining people's lives and their newspapers, too. #21 elbowed Tommy DiMicci on the court and got away with it. Tommy tried to yell something, but got lost in the sneaker shuffle and gave up without much of a fight, although it didn't slip by Rat Tail.

"You're a bitch, Number 21!" he yelled, "you're a bitch and your girlfriend knows it." The ref circled back and over and gave Rat Tail the slightest glimpse of attention, which was lethal. "Call the foul!" Rat Tail yelled. He got louder and louder, snapping his whip in the air, so worked up that the players got distracted.

"You can't do that!" he yelled. "Number 21, you cant just be a little bitch! Foul!" He turned it into to two distinct syllables. "Fow-ull! Fow-ull!" Two players passed the ball back and forth until #21 had enough and lunged at Rat Tail. He pushed him against the gym wall and got ready to punch him.

"Why don't you go to Jupiter to get more stupider," he yelled like a little baby bitch. His teammates peeled him off and away before anything got worse as Coach raced over to wrangle Rat Tail up. Before he made it to the hoop, Rat Tail tried for one last cheap shot and took off towards #21's back with a crumpled up fist, but three steps into his jog, the jump rope whip got tangled up all around his feet and everything took a turn for the worst. "Boy Trips And Falls." "Chin Breaks Fall." "Skin Slides Straight Off." "Raw Tissue From Lip To Neck; Boy Loses Front Tooth After Initiative Strikes Again."

All the women and the children screamed. The Dance Team said a prayer and winced and shuddered and shook. Rat Tail managed to sit up and lay back, his paper beard soaked in red and his eyes wild as his chin skin flapped against his Adam's apple. Somewhere in the chaos, his hands searched the floor for his tooth. All the Booster Moms dialed 911 at once. Number 21 got benched, finally. So did everybody else.

THE NECK BRACE DIDN'T LOOK HALF BAD. IT HAD A CERTAIN SERENITY to it that Rat Tail never had on his own. No movement, not a word. In the ambulance, Coach filled the silence and traced red semicircles on the knees of his khakis. He listened to the EMTs guestimate how old Mrs. Jarvis could possibly be by now. They went on about how crazy it was that anybody would ever trust anybody with that kind of liability. Coach nodded along, a brief smile, before locating his own student's tooth tangled up in his shoelaces. He picked it off and put its rough edges in Rat Tail's dangling stretcher hand. He held onto his palm for the briefest moment.

Rat Tail curled his knuckles up and turned it into a weak fist bump.

Coach tried to think of somebody to call, tried to find it within himself to step outside of himself, and do what was best for Rat Tail for once. He took a while to choose a number, and when he did, the call went straight to voice mail.

"Hello," he said. "This is Coach Henry from Freedom Point Junior High and I'm here with Rat Tail, on the way to the hospital, because his chin fell off. I just wanted to call and let you know that you can go fuck yourself because I've emailed you about 25 photos of my player, who is currently drenched in his own blood, and none of them have made it to print because your whole staff has been such little baby bitches. Have a terrible weekend, you assholes. Thank you." The ambulance went quiet. Rat Tail sighed and swallowed hard, a lispy whisper eventually surfacing. Coach leaned in close then sunk back into his seat.

"Totally," he said.

Boobs

The Jews crossed the Red Sea so that Jacob Kentor could finally go to Hooters.

And he did—after Bar Mitzvah—after Hebrew school and Talmud flashcards. After *please be seated*, Torah Aliyah, after Kleenex, after *Mazel Tov*, after Nana Rochelle's forehead kiss. After buffet banquet pizza slice and disc jockey with a goatee. After inflatable guitars and "Kokomo" on the dance floor. After the girl who may or may not be related to Walt Disney didn't show. After Jacob's heart broke for the first time. After slow dance with the needy girl by default. After Rabbi said, "Go on and be gracious," Jacob Kentor went to Hooters after school on a Monday.

For years, Jacob heard rumors about the Promised Land in the locker room during gym. It was one of the last chain restaurants in town, if you could even call it that—*a restaurant*. It was so much more than that. The men of Eighth Grade always showed up with t-shirts from their birthday dinners, all marked up with buffalo sauce and sharpie signatures from girls who added hearts and smileys to their names. They all looked the same, all the t-shirts, all the signatures. One Eighth Grader said that all the women gave him their phone numbers and that he could text them whenever he wanted, even if they didn't always text back. All the guys knew who Stacey was. None of them seemed to know how to describe her boobs. Jacob longed to be involved in that timeless struggle, and as he readied himself for manhood, his parents decided not to totally suck for once and let him join the brotherhood of wings—as long as he wasn't alone.

That's how PJ Sotheby got involved, even though he definitely wasn't a man.

PJ carried a flannel handkerchief on his belt loop and called it a snot rag but everybody knew it was part of a baby blanket. It was like he got younger with age. In Sixth Grade, PJ was all right because his parents still lived together. Then they split up and he became a wuss about everything. In Seventh Grade, on the trip to the Chippewa Natural History Museum, PJ wouldn't walk through the exhibit about birds because he didn't want to know where chicken nuggets came from. It was stupid, and he was stupid, but Jacob had to take someone to Hooters and PJ's dad was the most okay with the whole deal:

In honor of my *his birthday, Jacob will choose 1-3 friends for a trip to*

Hooters at 2:50 on Monday, May 2. Nobody go anywhere alone. Not even the bathroom. Everybody gets SIX wings and ONE soda. Free refills. No beer.

That's what the permission slip said. Jacob's mom signed the bottom and she made three copies for him to hand out at school. George, Chris, and the DiMicci twins all said no in their moms' handwriting. Mom made three more copies, then another six or so, and by the end of the week, all of Freedom Point Junior High and their moms knew that Jacob's mom thought it was okay for children to go to Hooters and just do whatever they want. Some kids didn't even come to the Bar Mitzvah after the permission slips went out. The girl who may or may not be related to Walt Disney was, for one, *very grossed out* and, therefore, definitely not *maybe or maybe not* flirting anymore. The only girl that showed at the party was the needy girl who got weird off of too many kiddie cocktails. PJ showed up to the ceremony and the party, both uninvited, just because he found an invitation in the school library and worried that people might talk about him if he wasn't there. He spent most of the night near Jacob's mom and told her she was very beautiful and warm and that Jacob was lucky to have her. He said he had never seen a woman with so much hair and that she looked like Black Beauty but with nicer teeth. By the end of the night, Jacob's mom gave PJ a permission slip and let him choose a keepsake from her purse. Jacob watched him rifle through a pocket of used up handkerchiefs during the limbo. In his three hours as a man, he had never seen anything dumber.

PJ was still dumb by the time Monday rolled around. Jacob tried to ignore the second handkerchief on PJ's belt loop as kids walked between the two of them at the after school pickup. Everybody slammed the doors on their parents' SUVs as Jacob watched PJ sneeze and then try to decide which handkerchief to use. The girl who may or may not be related to Walt Disney stepped off the curb with her friends as they passed by. Then the girl looked at Jacob and pretended to barf. All the girls congratulated themselves for being so funny in girl whispers. Jacob took his backpack off and turned to face PJ, who wiped his snot with his bare arm.

"Listen," Jacob said. "This is supposed to be a guys day for men only because that's just what it is and I could have chosen a cell phone instead of this, but I chose this because this is what men do and I have waited a very long time to do this, so if you feel like you don't want to do this because it's too grown up for you, then that's fine, we can all just go home, and, like, wait for everyone to not totally suck all the time." Jacob picked up his backpack and put it back on. He turned to face the street again. PJ wiped something out of his eye and rubbed the handkerchief ring with the palm of his hand. He slid the scraps out of the way and pulled some dumb note out of his pocket, bending down to the ground to flatten out all the corners. When he stood up, he cleared his throat.

"I found this in the trash. I think a girl wrote it." He said the second part again a little softer and held it up and winced a little. Jacob turned back just to roll his eyes and caught a glimpse of the signature purple lowercase pen ink that may or may not be related to Walt Disney. Typical girls always trying to make noise about nothing. Post-breakup whatever.

"PJ, you gotta be real dumb to just go digging through the trash, you know. That's not something you should just do, you probably got some stupid disease."

"I didn't," PJ whined, "I said I found it *near* the trash."

"Whatever."

"I don't even *like* the trash…"

"I said whatever, PJ. Just be a pussy to yourself." Two wannabe thugs walked by smoking pretzel rods as PJ kept rustling the note around his hands. It still sounded crispy, couldn't be that old. The Walt Disney girl probably went on and on about nothing at all. She probably just drew pictures of her dumb camp friends or her dance team or her dumb cousin that sold beaded lizard key chains to raise money for endangered teacup pigs. Not that Jacob was listening or whatever. PJ rustled his way closer and closer to Jacob on the curb.

"You want me to read it?"

"No."

"Because your name is in it 13 times, I counted."

"Good for you." Jacob moved into the street as a mini van approached.

Mom rolled up to the curb and ducked down behind the wheel. She wore sunglasses and a sweatshirt hood and rolled the windows down as she slowed to a stop. She shout-whispered at the boys to get in the car. That's who she was after the permission slips went out. It was very dumb, among other things.

PJ waved with his whole body and called Mom *Mom* like it was okay.

"I didn't know you were coming!" he said. "I would've brought my haiku poem, I got a B, because there's always room to grow!" Mom took her sunglasses off and gave PJ a round of applause. Jacob took his backpack off and tried not to implode from embarrassment.

"Where's dad?"

"He couldn't get away, another one of those crash diet patients." Jacob rubbed the back of his neck and let out a long sigh. Everything sucked. PJ spoke and it got even worse.

"I didn't know your dad was a doctor." Jacob crossed in front to the car door, mumbling under his breath.

"He's not, he's a nurse."

PJ sat shotgun and gave Mom a hug. He asked her to buckle his seatbelt while Jacob searched his bag in the back and started detangling his headphones.

"Can you just drop us at the drugstore?" he said. Mom slid her hood off.

"Are you sure?" That wasn't in the permission slip."

"Nobody gets dropped off by their mom at Hooters," Jacob said. "Unless they're a baby. Just drop us at the drugstore, we'll walk the extra blocks."

Mom took to the road as PJ started talking about how his dad was probably going to miss him a lot because usually he visited his dad's firm after school and waited for him in the lobby. Jacob put his headphones on and pretended not to hear him. He watched kids out the window hit each other with backpacks on the street corner. Near Park Place, some kids tried to feed a squirrel a piece of a bike tire. PJ felt the need to interrupt.

"Mom, I found a note about Jacob in the trash." He was such a little bitch.

"I thought you said it was *near* the trash."

"Yeah that's what I said, *near* the trash." Mom went off about how PJ should be a CSI or something equally not true because that's just the kind garbage that Moms have to talk about to feel alive. PJ made a slow move towards his front pocket.

"You wanna see what it says? I'll read it, I don't mind!"

"No," Jacob said. "If my name's in it, I get to say, and I say no." Mom stopped at a light while PJ balled the note back up. His voice got all whiny.

"Well why not? Don't you wanna know what she said?"

"*She*?" Mom said it in her snoopy mom voice.

"Yeah," PJ said, "do you know who Walt Disney is?" Jacob kicked the back of the passenger seat and PJ yelped. He rubbed his shoulders up and down like all the bones were broken or something dumb like that.

"What gives?" He said it so high, like a dog whistle or something.

"We're not talking about the note, I don't care about the note, because privacy is privacy and today is guys day. Guys don't gossip. Unless you're not a guy." PJ looked over at Mom and let out a long whimper cry.

"I'm a boy," he said, all sad and helpless, fishing for a hug or something.

Mom rubbed PJ's head as Jacob rolled his eyes so hard his ears popped. In that moment, it was clear—it was a long, long road to paradise.

While the rest of the car sang along to a radio jingle, Jacob got lost in the landscape outside his window. A group of girls ate dandelion leaves near Butternut Square. A kid near the west side stoplight walked with his mom to Freedom Point Diner. Jacob felt bad for him because he remembered what it was like to not be an adult and it was totally the worst. He felt sorry for his friends that had the dumbest parents ever. He felt sorry for the girl who may or may not be related to Walt Disney because, by the end of the day, she would just be some girl who didn't even compare to the real women of Hooters. He felt sorry for himself because he wasted six months trying to impress such a dumb nobody.

"You know," PJ said, turning around in his car seat. "If Mom wants to come with us, that'd be okay with me."

"Right here is fine," Jacob said. "Just drop us up here on the right."

Mom pulled the front tire up on grassy median in front of the drugstore and put the car in park. Jacob zipped his headphones up and PJ unbuckled as Mom started digging through her purse. She pulled an envelope out that said **NOT MONEY** and talked into the mirror.

"You take this and be extra careful. My treat."

"Right," Jacob said. "We'll call you."

PJ said thanks about a dozen times before finally getting out. He waved goodbye from the curb and Jacob watched the van get smaller and smaller on down the road. When it disappeared, Jacob surveyed the land. PJ clung to a lamppost and asked if cars ever drive up on sidewalks. Everything seemed faster and louder than in the car. For a brief moment, Jacob struggled to remember which way they should go. He wondered if his mom might loop back and point them in the right direction, but when it didn't happen, Jacob and PJ just started walking until it made sense. Near the town bog, they passed a China Express.

"I ate there once with my mom," PJ said. He said it again when Jacob didn't respond. "Over there, I ate there with my mom once."

"What do you want, a medal?"

"It was noodles, but not like macaroni. It was slimy, but not like macaroni. The sauce was called something weird. I don't really know, but you should get it some time. I don't really know what it was though, but I can ask my mom when I see her again." Jacob kicked rocks while PJ started sounding out nonsense words, trying to jog his memory. He finally got quiet after a few minutes. When he started up again, he almost whispered.

"You think she's coming back?"

"Who?"

"Mom."

"Which one?"

"Mine."

"I don't know, PJ. I don't even know her."

"Yeah but one time she said that she deserved somebody better and in the note I found, that's what it said about you, so I figured—" Jacob smacked PJ on the back of the head. His eyes got wide in shock, like it wasn't already coming to him.

"I said shut up about the note already. You got a lot of nerve to just do whatever you want after I was nice enough to let you be a guy for the day." PJ's voice cracked as he whined under his breath.

"But we aren't guys, we're boys."

"No PJ, I'm a man, and you're a baby."

"Says who?"

"Says me." PJ stayed real quiet after that, all torn up over nothing. Jacob worried that if he started crying, somebody would think he hit him and Hooters wouldn't happen. He tried to muster up all his energy to say one nice thing to clear the air and keep PJ going. It was very difficult.

"You say a lot of garbage without thinking PJ. That's probably why your mom left."

"Probably," PJ whispered, all dumb and sad.

"But you gotta just grow up, just be a man, just, I don't fricking know. Look at a baseball card or something and be that person. You gotta just take care of your own self now."

"I know," PJ said. "My dad already told me."

The sun felt hotter and higher as they went, but Jacob didn't want to bring it up because he didn't want to give PJ the impression that they were going to keep talking about stuff. After a block or two, Jacob started to sweat and PJ started singing a Disney song to himself. At that point, Jacob knew he should have chosen the cell phone.

When he stopped by the Old Dairy Queen to tie his shoe, PJ started up again.

"I heard about Stacey. She sounds, like, real nice," he said.

Jacob didn't say anything back, which PJ took as a cue to start asking about the girl who may or may not be related to Walt Disney. He yammered on about how she probably wouldn't even be that pretty if they lived in a bigger town because his dad said that his mom was *very* pretty until they moved from St. John's to Freedom Point and the population got a little bigger and that's why they're divorced. PJ said the last part a couple of times, a little quieter each time.

"That's why they're divorced. That's why."

PJ had something in his eye the rest of the walk. He didn't say much, which was fine because there wasn't much else to say. The girl who may or may not be related to Walt Disney *wasn't* that pretty. In fact, maybe she was ugly or fat compared to a super model. Not that it mattered. Just around the corner was a place full of very cute *and* hot *and* skinny *women* who were too grown up to be as dumb as the Seventh Grade girls of Freedom Point Junior High. The women were all there just waiting to touch Jacob on the shoulder and say things like "yes master" and "of course" and "I kiss on the first date." They definitely wouldn't let him down, that's for fricking sure. PJ interrupted Jacob's daydream.

"I see it," he said. Jacob looked back at PJ's outstretched arm. Both boys stopped and squinted as PJ spoke again, almost breathless. "There it is."

Jacob looked on. Two dogs barked at a stray orange balloon three corners up near a gas station. He followed the balloon with his eyes as it drifted higher, up and up, up into the clouds, smaller and smaller until the glow of an orange sign distracted him. It was bigger and brighter than the rest of Freedom Point, and almost not even *in* Freedom Point, almost on the other side of bordering St. John's. In his 23 hours as a man, it was literally the most beautiful thing that Jacob had ever seen.

Without saying anything, the boys took off in a sprint. Their backpacks hit each other until PJ saw a flower and felt the need to announce that he was going to stop to pick it. Jacob kept on and started to feel sorry for the sort of Walt Disney girl again. In his last few steps, Jacob fell into a slow jog and then walked it off on the front lawn of the restaurant. He replayed everything that all the Eighth Graders had said and thought about the commercials he had seen—all the guys-guys packed around the bar for the big game. Women with beer or a beverage of your choice. Boobs and loud music. And boobs. $20 bills. Michael Jordan was in one of the commercials. He'd probably gone there like a billion times because all the women touched his shoulder and not just anybody gets to touch Michael Jordan. Michael Jordan probably *loved* Hooters because Hooters was what it was all about: A real life party with real life babes who all aimed to please all the grownup guys-guys—Jacob, now, included.

When PJ finally caught up on the restaurant lawn, both of them adjusted their backpacks and combed their hair with their hands. Sweat was everywhere, for every reason. The lawn smelled like onion rings. Jacob and PJ both got real quiet and headed for the entryway. Right in front of an ashtray, PJ asked Jacob if he wanted to see the flower that he picked. It was literally the worst timing.

When Jacob opened the Hooters door, a wave of air conditioning and barbecue musk washed over him, and the place was so dark that he almost couldn't see. PJ stood behind him and held onto his backpack zipper until they made it through the foyer and Jacob told him to lay off. When they got inside, neither of them said a word.

The walls were made of dark hardwood, like somebody stapled tree bark in giant sheets, and old dusty photos of girls with big hair were tacked up around the room. All of them seemed to be on a different angle. There was a plant in every corner and one still had a price tag. Somebody left a crayon with a bite out of it on the hostess stand. Two guys with eye patches sat at a table near the price tag plant and one of them seemed to be hiding a pile of crab leg shells under his chair. People clapped on TV for a golf channel putt. A fat guy in a polo shirt did a crossword by the bar register. He was almost big enough to be taken away in an ambulance for just being. The people at the hospital probably knew all about him. Dad would probably have the scoop. It'd probably be a good story, whenever things finally slowed down and he had the chance to come home. An A.C. unit buzzed in a nearby corner, before shorting out and smoking a little bit. Jacob felt instantly cold, his sweat freeze-dried. PJ's teeth chattered by his ear.

"Do we seat ourselves?" he said. Jacob spoke without moving his mouth.

"I don't know."

"Should we call your mom?"

"No," Jacob said. "Why would we go home?" PJ got even closer.

"This place looks like murderers," he whispered. His hand hit Jacob's thigh as he massaged his belt of handkerchiefs. Jacob took a few steps towards the fat man at the register and cleared his throat. The one eye patch guy repositioned his feet to hide his stash of shells. Somebody had a good swing on the green on TV. Jacob cleared his throat again and waited for the fat guy to look up. PJ interrupted.

"Is Stacey here?" he said real loud. He held his flower out and looked dumb. Jacob couldn't believe that PJ believed in *anything* that the guys said anymore, let alone what they said about Stacey. He wondered which one of them had the balls to make the whole thing up. He wondered if Stacey was code for something else. He wondered if those kids back near Park Place finally got the squirrel to eat that piece of the bike tire. Somebody missed an important swing on TV. Jacob pulled PJ's backpack strap and turned to leave.

"Sure," the fat guy said. "Stacey's here." The boys stopped moving.

"*She is?*" PJ said. "Um. Okay." Nobody said anything else.

"So…do you want me to get her?" the fat guy said. PJ turned to Jacob who took a deep breath and rolled his eyes.

"Whatever," he said.

"Sure!" PJ said. He said it a few times, getting louder each time. "Unless she's busy." Jacob watched the fat guy look around the dining room. The eye patch guys laughed at the pants that the TV golfers were wearing. The fat guy shrugged.

"Nope," he said. "Got an hour before dinner rush, I'll give her a holler. You boys want to take a seat?"

Jacob and PJ crossed over to a barstool table and climbed up to sit down. The fat guy disappeared into the back. He poked his head out and yelled across the room a moment later.

"You want me to give her that?" He pointed at PJ's hand and the messed up flower. PJ looked across the table.

"Can I stop and get another one for your mom?" he said.

"Whatever," Jacob said. "I don't know." He rolled his eyes so hard that it hurt. PJ leaned over and held his hand out to the fat guy.

"I guess so," he yelled. The fat guy looked even fatter as he got closer and took the stem. Jacob had never seen anyone so fat in his adult life. If that was the face of Hooters, he didn't even want to know what somebody in the back looked like. Stacey probably didn't have a leg or something. Or she probably had a Siamese twin and that's how those guys got so many signatures. Not that the signatures meant anything anyway. The Eighth Graders probably never even went to Hooters. *And why would Michael Jordan lie like that?* Jacob felt sorry for himself while PJ read a menu.

"Do you think the children's quesadilla is spicy?" he asked.

"We're not staying," Jacob said. PJ looked all sad and dumb.

"We aren't?" he said. "Then why'd we sit down?"

"I don't know," Jacob said. "Because my backpack hurts."

"It does?" PJ said. "Because mine hurts too but I didn't want to say anything because I didn't know if you would know what I was meaning when I did." PJ kept yammering on and being the worst until Jacob couldn't take it anymore and put his head on the table. He rubbed his eyes with his fingertips until PJ suddenly stopped mid-sentence. Jacob lifted his head and let his eyes refocus, and PJ looked two shades more wussed-out than usual. Jacob assumed a spider had walked by or the museum eagle had returned, but when he rotated on his stool towards the kitchen, all of his insides unraveled. She was real.

Every step she took was in slow motion and when she moved, Jacob swore he heard a guitar solo that was literally the coolest. Her hair was as beautiful as a golden retriever and it was big and it was all in a pile on her boobs. The men of Eighth Grade were right. There wasn't a word for those. Not even in Hebrew. Her t-shirt fit very good. So did her shorts and her butt. Not that Jacob was looking. Her legs and her face looked like she had just gone somewhere hot like Hawaii and got a suntan. Her face had plenty of makeup on it, but not the kind all the dumb Seventh Graders bought from the movie theater bathroom machines. Real stuff, like colors that a clown would use. Like turquoise. As she got closer, she smiled, holding PJ's stupid flower. It was such a slap in the face to give a woman like that a flower so dumb. The worst. Thank god he had Jacob around. Stacey was so sexy that Jacob had to put his backpack on his lap and recite his Haftarah to settle down. Then Stacey smiled. He was done for.

"Which one of you do I thank for this?" She held the weed up to her face and took a big smell. What a woman. Jacob looked at PJ and hoped he was rubbing his handkerchief loop under the table.

"B-both of us" Jacob said. "It's…we got it for you." Stacey took another whiff and put the flower on the table. Then she reached out and put a hand on Jacob's shoulder. One of her nails had a Playboy bunny on it. Her boobs had almost nothing on them. Stacey smiled at both sides of the table.

"You two are the sweetest guys I know." Jacob lowered his chin into his neck and forced his voice to get deeper.

"I know you are but what am I?" he said. Stacey just laughed because she was the best and skinny and pretty. Jacob could barely remember the name of the girl who may or may not be related to Walt Disney. Not that it mattered. Finally, a real woman who could keep up with a real man had arrived.

"What are you gentlemen drinking?" she said. She pulled a notepad from the waistband of her shorts. Classic Stacey.

"Do you have bottled water?" PJ said.

"We want Pepsi," Jacob said. "We'll both just have Pepsi." Stacey scribbled on the pad without even looking. So her.

"And wings," Jacob said. "We both want six wings."

"How hot do you want them?" She was such a tease and she was hot enough to be in every music video.

"How hot is mild?" PJ asked.

"We want them as hot as you can make them," Jacob said. "Whatever other guys get, that's how we eat ours."

"Your wish is my command," she said and Jacob readjusted his backpack as his lap got hotter. It didn't even feel physically possible to look her in the eyes anymore. Stacey turned back halfway across the floor. "Don't you go anywhere" she said. She moved her hips back to the kitchen. PJ and Jacob both sighed.

"I like her personality a lot," PJ said. "They don't make them like that anymore." Jacob didn't say anything back because there wasn't much else to say. She *did* have a great personality. *And* boobs. And she didn't have to call her mom or sign a permission slip or do any of the stupid stuff that dumb, flakey, Seventh Graders of Freedom Point Junior High had to do. She was free. She was real. She showed up and when she did, she chose Jacob's shoulder to touch. There, on the other side of town, after what felt like years of wandering, Jacob had finally become a man.

PJ blew bubbles in his soda as Jacob started talking.

"Hey, what else did it say?"

"What did *what* say?"

"The note, what else did it say." PJ smiled all dumb and big and burrowed his way back into his pocket. The ball looked all soft and warm as he unwrapped it. PJ pointed to smeared purple ink spots as he gave a play by play. One part had a ketchup stain on it. The note definitely came from inside the garbage.

"She says that her camp friends know about the time you got your ear pierced and it got infected and she doesn't feel bad for telling them."

"What a bitch."

"Yeah totally," PJ said. "She's a witch and a real mean person and, like all of that stuff."

"What else?"

"She says that she doesn't like-like you anymore, but if you buy her a necklace, she'll reconsider it, so."

"What a bitch,"

"Yeah, but, like, for really." PJ rolled his eyes and started bubbling again. He scrunched the straw wrapper into a worm and then spoke real slow.

"So…are you gonna buy her one?" It was actually the dumbest.

"PJ, you need to try thinking before you say crap."

"Okay," he said real soft.

When the wings arrived, Stacey touched Jacob's shoulder again and told him to enjoy before disappearing. PJ wussed out and wiped the sauce off his wings with a table napkin. Jacob ripped through the wings until he couldn't feel his face anymore. Then he pulled the leftovers apart so that Stacey would think he ate those ones too. When she came back to check on them, he said he was doing great even though his insides were very likely on fire. She touched his shoulder again before departing.

"I think she likes us," PJ said. "I bet she'll talk about us after we leave, but like in a real good way, like she misses us almost."

"Whatever," Jacob said. He almost started to feel bad for PJ in that moment, but something stopped him. Then Stacey came back and Jacob remembered what it was.

"Stacey," PJ said. "Do you like us?"

PJ was literally the absolute worst.

"You know, I'm not supposed to play favorites here at Hooters," Stacey said with her arms crossed and a dramatic pout. "Because then feelings get hurt."

"Duh," Jacob said, "Why would you even ask that?"

"I don't know, " PJ said. "I say a lot of things without really thinking." Stacey laughed and played with her notepad.

"That's okay," she said. "I work with a lot of people who say a lot of things without thinking." God. She was so wise or pretty or both. Jacob watched her look around the restaurant. The eye patch guys were gone and a trail of crab leg shells traced their route to the door. Stacey leaned in and lowered her voice.

"You wanna know a secret?" she said. Her eyes got bigger and all the creases on her lids filled up with extra turquoise shadow. She tucked her notepad in the back waistband of her shorts and PJ and Jacob leaned in.

"I *really* like you guys," she said. "Probably more than any guys that have come in all week." PJ leaned forward on his barstool.

"More than all the boys that come in, too?"

"Yes," she said, "All the boys, too." PJ took a deep breath and sighed and smiled in relief. Stacey put her hand on Jacob's shoulder. By the end of the meal, she'd probably do it at least half a dozen times. Being a man was the opposite of suck. Being a man ruled. Stacey looked around the restaurant again, rising up on the tips of her white sneakers to check every corner of the place. She leaned back in and whispered.

"Do you wanna know why I like you guys so much?" she said. Jacob thought it was nice that Stacey kept including PJ in on his seduction.

What a woman. Class, that what she had. PJ showed all his teeth and nodded as fast as he could. Jacob played it very cool while getting ready to adjust his backpack on his lap again. Stacey slid her Playboy bunny nail from the front of her waistband to the back, and pulled her notepad out again. She fluttered her eyelashes and flipped to the very back, page by page. She smiled before sliding the notepad on the table. Jacob didn't take his eyes off her face until she opened her mouth.

"Do you wanna know why?" she said again. She tapped her finger and Jacob let his eyes drop. Taped to the back of the notepad was a Polaroid of a boy Jacob seen around school.

"You remind me of my son," she said. Jacob watched PJ's eyes fill up with tears of joy. His elbow moved around as he played with his handkerchief loop. Stacey asked if he was alright and PJ smiled his stupid smile and said he was so honored that she would say something like that because having a mom is so great and not everybody gets to see their mom all the time because sometimes moms stay in St. John's with Charlie from next door.

"But I'm just a boy," he said. "so she's still got time to come back." Stacey nodded along and made an equally stupid face, while Jacob felt tiny on his barstool. After all that work—after Hebrew School, Talmud flashcard. After please be seated, Torah Aliyah, after six-block drugstore walk for freedom, Jacob's heart broke for the second time. Stacey tied a table napkin onto PJ's stupid belt loop as Jacob let his voice return to its normal pitch.

"Do you have a phone?" he said. He couldn't take his eyes off the Polaroid.

"Sure," she said, "just ask Tony, sweetheart." She motioned with her neck to the bar while PJ laid his head on her arm. Jacob monkeyed his way off his stool and crossed the floor in fast motion. The fat guy in the polo stacked cups of ranch dressing and fiddled with the lids. He looked bigger than ever, maybe even older. Jacob asked for a phone and when the guy handed it to him, he wondered if the girl who may or may not be related to Walt Disney might be home. He wondered how much a necklace would cost. He started dialing and his mom picked up.

"I'm almost ready," he said.

"Okay," she said. "I'm on my way. Walgreen's."

"You can just come here, out front, it doesn't matter."

"Okay," Jacob's mom said. "But warn all the men that a girl is coming."

Jacob nodded and took a look around the restaurant. He wondered where they all might be.

The Ballad of Lauren Price

WHEN LAUREN PRICE REALLY LISTENED, IT ALL SOUNDED A LOT LIKE this: fast blood through a plastic bag or a water balloon full of feelings. Heartbeat rhythm gallop and violin whisper. Bedroom speaker rumble over mom and dad, who made noise in the basement studio, rewarding a new class of scene study wannabes that believed that the Price School For Theatrical Stardom was a real deal ticket to Hollywood.

Back upstairs, in Lauren's room, a noisy silence, a track change, and a song about being seen and cherished and wanted. When Lauren Price really listened, it sounded a lot like Spanish cologne and it felt like soft massage and real gold chain and open ears and glimmering eyes. Total effing undivided attention. That's what Paolo Sonata's new album sounded like.

If anybody needed proof, Lauren Price could vouch. She had listened to Paolo Sonata for 698 days straight, had fallen in love with him when she first heard his voice on an episode of *Miami Top Model: In Or Out:*

The Final Footage: The Making of a Dream. Those were simpler times, the golden age of 11, before boobs came in and braces came off and everybody lost their g.d. minds. That was when mom and dad started the school and made all the money and left the parenting and the grocery shopping to Esmeralda, and, in an attempt to be known for something other than her parents' fame, Lauren started lying. Big lies. Good ones, too. In a single week, she booked a McDonald's ad in Rome and was approached by a detective that said she may or may not be related to Walt Disney.

Still, the people of Freedom Point, Wisconsin were hard to please. Even Lauren's best friends, Crystal&Krystal, only pretended to care in order to buy more time to drop hints about how *they* might want to model, too, and, *say*, maybe Lauren's mom and dad could get them in because everybody in Freedom Point knew that Lauren's mom and dad had been in a big time movie with Brad Pitt for almost a whole 26 seconds. They played waiters. Amish waiters.

Lauren played along, reluctantly. That's what it meant to be a Price, whether you liked it or not. Mom and dad and the business of stardom came first. Then the feelings of anybody paying for stardom. Then the feelings of people that weren't even paying for stardom but still felt the need to be little bitches, like when Crystal&Krystal got all defensive anytime Lauren told them that they weren't, actually, really that good at anything, let alone imaginary modeling.

"You're just jealous that we have potential," they'd once said. "Where's your Amish costume? What have you done lately?"

What an effing joke. They were both too broken to have potential. They didn't even go by their real names. If anybody had potential as an imaginary model, it was Lauren. She was already *booking* gigs as an imaginary model. Still, at a certain point, Lauren stopped trying to prove anything to anyone and kept her mouth shut and passed along another dozen amateur headshots. There was no point in being honest. The people of Freedom Point just wanted what they wanted, and it was rarely Lauren.

That's why it was almost physically painful to listen Paolo. He was so nice to without asking for anything. He was so special, the way he talked about el amor verdadero in "Beso Beso Beso." The kind of magic he had, the way he could reel you in. Lauren dreamt of having an anthem of her own, having anything to say—or said about her—that was so incredible that all the needy trolls of Freedom Point would finally shut their mouths and just admire. Some nights, she made imaginary lists of all the things she could announce that would make her seem cooler or hotter or permanently remarkable. The modeling contract. The Disney thing. An extra invisible boob that boys would have to buy jewelry to see. Every scheme worked for a day or two until people eventually lost interest in being nice.

Two could play that game, though.

THAT'S WHY, IN A STROKE OF TOTAL EFFING GENIUS, ON A PARTICULARLY boring Tuesday night, to the background track of "Mas Mas Mas," Lauren Price took a deep breath and spontaneously caught cancer.

WORD SPREAD FAST. IT TORE THROUGH THE HALLS AND SLAMMED lockers shut, and as it found its way across campus, all of Freedom Point Junior High was forced to love Lauren but fear her but like her even though she was still sort of mean. If anything, the cancer made Lauren Price *meaner*, but everybody pretended not to notice. That's how great of a lie it was. All she had to do was tell Crystal&Krystal that some imaginary doctor up near Duluth wrote CANCER in big red letters on a file and told her that it was a tragedy, but she absolutely didn't get it because of her sexual activity which was *very* advanced for her age, even though she didn't talk about it all that much.

Crystal&Krystal seemed more jealous than sad when Lauren initially shared the news. They got real weird and huddled up on top of Lauren's comforter, while somebody threw a chair downstairs in the studio. Lauren thought Crystal&Krystal might cry or say something that they'd learned from a monologue workshop, but Crystal got real quiet and took her hands off the bed real slow, wiping them on her jeans as fast as she could.

"This is very crazy and dumb. Is it safe for us to be here? Can we catch it?"

"No," Lauren said.

"Are you retarded?" Krystal chimed. Crystal tried to look especially unretarded.

"Well what kind of cancer is it?" Lauren hadn't thought about that. She tried to remember what kind the girls always got in Nicholas Sparks movies, but when it didn't naturally come to her, she did what she always did and let the spirit of performance fill her until a new truth arrived. Advanced improvisation. The purest form of artistry.

"Earlobe," she said. "It's earlobe cancer, but like it's in my blood and stuff, so it's also more just like general cancer."

"*Earlobe?*" Crystal said. She looked like somebody told her a ghost or some kind of spider might be in the room. It was probably also shocking that she had actually listened to somebody say something for the first time in her life. "They're sure it's earlobe?" she said. She got real quiet after that, hush hush even. "*Can you still wear earrings?*"

"Probably not." Crystal&Krystal looked like *they* were ghosts at that point. They both took Lauren's hands and lowered their heads as mom and dad applauded for someone in the distance.

"We won't tell anyone," Krystal said.

The next day, Lauren's whole locker was filled with loose Skittles and sympathy cards and a crinkly notebook note from some Sixth Grade fatty she'd been actively trying to avoid. The fatty asked a bunch of questions about the cancer and if it was true, and then went on and on about how if it was, one of her friend's parakeets, Donatella, died of cancer, but Lauren would probably be okay, because the internet said that God only takes people away once they're full of lessons. That was page one of twelve.

The fatty was probably making the whole thing up for undeserved attention. She probably read about it in a Chicken Soup for whatever book. She probably didn't even *have* a friend with a parakeet, let alone one named Donatella. Lauren could play that game. After school, she traced her way through the entire student body to the fatty, who ate Skittles on the floor in the corner of the library, a whole handful of red ones, like she'd fished all the good ones out before filling Lauren's locker up. Little biotch.

As Lauren approached, the fatty looked even more desperate, rounder, too, like a bowling ball wearing overalls or something. She curled her weird little nubs over the rest of the candy as Lauren stopped right in front of her, a hush over the rest of the room. Total silence. Even the librarian. Completely weird, but equally effing amazing. Lauren waited for Crystal&Krystal to lose interest like they always did, to slip off on some weird pose-off between the two of them, but they didn't. It was almost like they were really listening. Yeah right. Very good scene work. The fatty wasn't nearly as slick.

"Your eyeliner looks so pretty up close," she said. "Could you show me how to do it? Do you wanna hangout? Is it true that you're dying? I have a coupon for Pizza Wagon, if you want to split a corner piece." Lauren took a moment to center herself before delivering an honest rejection with just a touch of compassion.

"What are you, retarded?" she said. "Don't you know, *I'm a model in Japan*, I can't have pizza. I only drink coconut water with a little piece of fish food in it."

"I know," the fatty said, some slow nod creeping up on her as everybody waited for confirmation. "But I just thought that maybe you could let me help you, because I can learn how to be a friend, too" and on and on, whatever. It was totally rude, whatever it was. Here Lauren was, hypothetically dying, and, still, the fatty felt the need to use up her time on some long scene that didn't really have any point or anything. When she started to talk even softer, lower, her face all dumb and sad, Lauren made a last minute choice in body language and slapped the fatty's hand. Two Skittles rolled out and Lauren picked them off the floor and put them in her mouth. She chewed them up, her hands all wild as she tried to pull her own mouth open while eating, but it didn't work. Her eyes grew wide as she swallowed. Crystal&Krystal gasped. So did everybody else. Even the librarian.

"Look at what you made me do!" Lauren yelled, "Why would you make me eat those after I told you I can't?" The fatty got all worked up and loud.

"What? I didn't, I mean, I, but, *you* put them in *your* mouth."

"Are you retarded? I don't eat Skittles, *I can't even eat pizza.* You threw them in my mouth!" Lauren started gasping and grabbed her throat, spit pooling all around her tongue. It was amazing. Everybody bought it because it was interesting and remarkable and a great use of space.

"I didn't mean to!" the fatty yelled. "You know I'm still learning people skills!" Crystal&Krystal ushered Lauren out of the room as they shamed the fatty for sparking what must've been some sort of cancer attack. Students started whispering as the fatty stayed and cried, trying to cover it up by untying and retying her shoes. Amateur choice. Lauren let out a long sigh.

"Ugh," she said. "My sister is so annoying."

THINGS ONLY WENT UP FROM THERE. ONCE WORD GOT OUT, THE whole school tried to hold Lauren's hand in a more appropriate fashion. People pushed fish flakes through the little grates in her locker and teachers finally let Lauren use purple gel pen on stuff even though it wasn't typically allowed. For some reason, Miss Cunningham was inspired to stop yelling at Lauren about texting in Foods class and she chose to spend her time making a bundt cake and crying about how everybody has an angel and hers was Whitney Houston and they would both be praying for Lauren's recovery. Awkward. Lauren's ex-whatever, Jacob, started saying "hey" again, which was whatever.

Some nobody teacher that had no life told Lauren that she should clear her situation with the nurse's office before anything got too out of hand, because, god forbid, something get out of hand at Freedom Point Junior High, home of the jealousies.

Getting proof of cancer was a challenge, if not just a completely retarded hassle. Lauren spent all evening trying to teach Esmeralda how to be a useful maid and how to say "cancer" into the phone receiver, but it simply wasn't in the cards. As people filed in the front door for scene study, she thought about asking one of them to call in and pretend that they were her mom or dad, but she knew they'd over do it. Lauren's mom and dad would never get all sloppy over anything. That's what it meant to be a Price. You pulled it together and maintained composure and you finished the job no matter what it took.

And if you couldn't finish it, you hired somebody like Esmeralda until you could.

Once class was in session, Lauren lingered by the studio door and listened to her parents demonstrate proper emotions. Loud wailing. Sugary excitement. It was comforting to know that they did, in fact, know how to feel those things even if they never showed it. Somebody sneezed near the door mid-session, which prompted a whispered "bless you" from the kitchen. Whoever it was wasn't very slick.

Lauren looked over her shoulder and struggled to see who it was in the shadows. A bag crinkled and she had a pretty good idea.

"If whoever said that doesn't come out right now, they're going to have to go back to Mexico with Esmeralda, and they'll never get their period, ever." A moment of silence passed and then, slowly, a bowling ball in overalls with a French braid crept out, holding a bag of chips.

"Are your friends here?" the fatty said.

"No."

"Do you want to hangout?"

Lauren rolled her eyes.

"Do you want to hangout?"

"I heard you the first time," Lauren said. "I'm busy."

"Oh. Okay."

The fatty waited around and ate chips, the bag all loud and crumpled. Mom and dad cooed like babies behind the door. The snack bag crinkled again.

"Do you think that's what they did when we were babies?" the fatty said. "I bet they loved us a lot when we were babies. Everybody loves babies."

"Don't you have somewhere to be?" Lauren said.

"No."

"Well can you find somewhere to be?" The fatty crinkled up the bag again and then got very quiet.

"Is it true, Lauren?"

"What?"

"The cancer stuff. I asked Esmeralda, but I don't think she understood.

Is it true?" Mom and dad told somebody in the studio to exercise honesty, or at least just fake it. The fatty swallowed hard, an audible gulp lingering in the air.

"No, Isabella, it's not true," Lauren said. "But if anybody asks at school, it is true."

"Yeah, okay."

"I mean it, Isabella, if you tell anybody, I'm gonna keep telling people you're adopted."

"Okay." Isabella started crinkling again and faded away, all the way across the house. Slowly, back again, closer and closer again, until Lauren could hear her pretending not to be back in the kitchen. The rustling fell completely silent again.

"What?" Lauren said.

"So..it's like *our* secret? The cancer?"

"No, Isabella, it's my secret, you just got in the way, apparently."

"Oh, okay," she said. "Well, you can count on me."

"Well, I should hope so."

When Isabella didn't leave, Lauren looked back to roll her eyes. Still, Isabella just stood there, leaning out of a shadow. A big stupid smile found its way across her face, like the time mom and dad said they'd make it to her birthday party, right before they actually didn't make it at all.

Lauren's phone buzzed from the seat of her pants and Crystal&Krystal

asked if she was still alive. Typical. They probably only wanted to know before they went somewhere else for annunciation lessons. Isabella found the courage to be bothersome one more time.

"Do your friends know about our secret?"

"No," Lauren said. "And it's not ours, it's mine."

"Oh yeah, okay." Isabella waited a few more seconds to build some kind of misinformed dramatic tension. "Well you can still count on me."

"You can go now," Lauren said. "Whatever."

By the time scene study let out, mom and dad were too tired to make any ambiguous phone calls or even tuck anyone in, so Lauren left it up to Paolo Sonata's "Vida Vida Vida: Part II." He was so kind to sweep in with smooth violins and yearning whisper and gentle butterfly wing kind of sadness that was so sincere and sexy and hot and cute and damaged all at once. She wondered how long it would take for the cancer to make her *that* interesting.

Not that it even mattered anymore. Isabella would probably mess the whole thing up. And if not her, somebody else. Other than Paolo, nobody was really on Lauren's side. Mom and dad couldn't care less and Crystal&Krystal had their own eating disorders to focus on and the nobody teacher made the whole school question the whole thing, anyways. That's what it really meant to be a Price in Freedom Point. You had to be let down by everybody, all the time.

Lauren turned her stereo down and a hallway light appeared underneath the door. Somebody barely knocked. A new crinkle followed, maybe a candy bar or jellybean bag. Lauren pretended to be asleep until it started up again. At the door, Isabella hid under a giant fleece blanket and extended a Ziploc bag full of hair.

"It's from my doll," she whispered. "But we could pretend it's yours. It said on the Internet that, sometimes, the cancer makes it fall off." She lifted her arm and put it next to Laurens forehead. "You can count on me," she said.

Lauren snatched the bag up and broke open the seal and ran her fingers through it. Isabella watched, so tired, yet seemingly so overcome with joy all at once. Lauren zipped it back up and handed over. As she started to close the door, she paused for a moment.

"Good job, or whatever."

BY MORNING, LAUREN HAD THE BRILLIANT IDEA OF ALSO FILLING UP another Ziploc bag with white Tic Tacs and smashing them up and writing CANCER MEDICINE in bold letters on the label. Isabella made a cameo in the nurse's office during the big time to shine, right before school.

"Is my sister here?" she said. She almost sang it, her blocking from some old chorus role she'd gotten because somebody dropped out and mom and dad needed balance on the stage. She held out the Tic Tac bag and shook the dust in front of the nurse. "This is my sister's cancer medication, because *she has cancer*, but it got broken in my backpack." That was Lauren's cue. *Broken*. From the hallway, she slouched over and shuffled in and interrupted.

"It's okay, I already talked to mom, and she said I'll just take it when I get home, because the cancer isn't going anywhere anyways." Lauren scratched her head, before revealing her palm, a handful of planted doll hair wisping to the floor in a light clump. A group of nearby students gasped. If there was ever time for an effing standing ovation, it was now.

The shame was that the whole performance was wasted on some new nobody. Nurse Katzler was on leave and left behind some young sub that was related to somebody important and smelled like burnt pennies. She panicked as the hair drifted across the rug and asked Lauren to take a seat and kicked the door shut. Isabella slunk her way off to first hour, back in the role of the fatty. When the coast was clear, the nurse sub asked Lauren if she had tried medical marijuana because it's not the problem, people are the problem.

"It's the people," she said, all worked up. "I can run it by a parent or physician of choice."

"No," Lauren said. It was pointless to even waste a good lie on that train wreck. "My doctor is a very private person and my parents own an acting school and I'm a model, so we can't be bothered with anything from the simpletons in this town." Lauren slipped into a southern accent on that last word, "simpletons." Remarkable natural choice.

"They were in that Brad Pitt movie," the sub nurse said. "Some of the best 26 seconds I've ever seen on screen, and I mean *ever.*" Lauren wondered how mom and dad found the time to outshine her in her own school, on her own deathbed.

"What can I say," Lauren said. "They know how to make an entrance and an exit." She paused and let out a long sigh. "I'll miss them when I'm dead."

"Of course," the sub nurse said. "I definitely get that." After Lauren left, the sub nurse sent out a memo to let everybody know that people needed to pull together, because cancer's not the problem, people are the problem.

The not-so-official-official-not-real-real-diagnosis whipped everybody into shape in no time. Nobody wasted breath asking Lauren for any more favors, not even Crystal&Krystal, who decided to focus their efforts on a cleanse diet they'd heard some Eighth Graders talking about. Most people went overboard with sympathy cards even though Lauren was still alive. Maybe even the most alive she'd ever been.

Things were even looking up for Isabella. Her weight started to yo-yo because she had something to do that didn't involve processed sugar.

Consolation headbands and lip-gloss started showing up in her locker and when she gave her class speech about helping verbs, everybody clapped, which was a very exciting development. Some people even stood up when they clapped, which almost never happened for Isabella *or* helping verbs. Rumor had it that some boy in the library even offered to kiss her if she thought it might take some of the grief away.

"He's not really my type," she'd said during a late-night make-under session. It was a special skill, the nausea green under Lauren's eyes. Isabella blended half a dozen eye shadows to get the right shade while she went on about how hard it was to find modern romance.

"I don't think I'm gonna kiss him because facts are facts. Everybody knows he's into moms, so I don't know if he really gets me."

"It's probably best," Lauren said, Paolo whispering in background speaker rumble. "We're busy enough as is." Isabella held Lauren's face and blended the same spot over and over again as she tried to hide a smile.

"Yeah," she said. "*We* are."

AFTER THE FIRST FEW WEEKS OF BLISSFUL DISEASE, PEOPLE STARTED TO crave updates at an alarming rate. When Lauren and Isabella weren't particularly clear, people assumed the worst. Soon, nearly everybody sported green under their eyes, real green, the sleepless kind, dark mustard circles. They all looked a little more ragged, like zombies and carsickness. Isabella thought it might be best time to do some backtracking because the whole thing didn't seem quite as fun anymore. Plus, the kissing guy wasn't half bad, so maybe that could be a thing. In the meantime, somebody got the idea to hand out memorial ribbons with Lauren's face under a halo and the word BELIEVE, which Lauren took as a cue to get sicker, whether Isabella liked it or not.

"Thank you to everyone," she said on the morning announcements. "Even those of you who are weird, I appreciate that you're showing up or something. I will keep fighting, because, as my idol Paolo Sonata says, 'Mas mas mas mas vida vida vida vida.' But just so everybody knows, it's not going good so like who really knows."

After the announcement, Isabella got especially worked up and interrupted Crystal&Krystal's "memorial fast" for a private word with Lauren.

"I thought we were gonna to start winding down," she said. "I thought that's what we decided."

"*We* aren't sick, I am." Lauren let out a long wet cough and Isabella started to look all wussed-up over it. "What, are you gonna cry?" Isabella scrunched her hands up, her nubs all red. 'You wanna hit me? Hit me. Then you'll really be a little biotch."

"I'll tell on you."

"Tell who? Esmeralda? What, you suddenly speak Mexican?"

"I'll tell mom and dad."

"I dare you to," Lauren said. "Maybe, while you're at it, you can remind them we were born." That was Isabella's breaking point. The red drained from her whole body and her lip quivered as she pulled an emergency Ziploc of Skittles from her back pocket and went to town. As she turned to leave, she said mumbled under her breath.

"My dolls and I hope you die."

IT WASN'T JUST ISABELLA WHO TOOK ACTION AFTER LAUREN'S announcement. All of Freedom Point Junior High started loving Paolo Sonata, too, with everything inside, with their time and their parents' money. Some teachers hung posters up with live pictures from the Hambre De Segundo Tour. Everybody learned the words to "Poesíai Sangre" in no time. The Eighth Grade girls and Crystal&Krystal finally found the strength to slim down into youth sized Paolo Sonata t-shirts because they were all attention hogs. Some wannabe started an after school club where all the other wannabes could meet and cry and carve his lyrics into the rubber on the sides of their sneakers, like that was going to help Lauren in any way. Even teachers started loving Paolo because he gave $1 from every copy of "Love Worship Angel Fuego" to poor people who needed books or something. Some of them used his music to talk about poetry or sexual reproduction or something equally unimportant. It was all completely amazing, but also effing retarded, as nobody liked Paolo until Lauren started dying.

The tipping point was the administration. Principal McPhee liked Paolo a lot because he said Paolo reminded him of his wife, even though he legally couldn't call her that anymore because she moved out and changed her name.

"It's been a hard year," he said, all awkward and sad and principal-y in his office.

"I know," Lauren said, a little ticked off, letting out her signature cough as a subtle reminder to get back to appropriate sympathy. Principal McPhee handed Lauren a tissue and then he started to cry, which was ugh.

That was the new trend, the unexpected breakdown. She had seen a lot of people cry at Freedom Point Junior High. They cried when she started wearing band-aids on her earlobes as a "preventative measure." They cried when she said she had to give up modeling because her look got *too real* and that's the business, so what can you do. They cried when she started wearing a bandana, her hair tucked underneath in little braids, and when she told the whole school on the morning announcements that Paolo Sonata came to her in some kind of weird distant dream and told her that she was still very hot even though she could, like, very well being dying. That was the day that all the teachers stopped caring if she did her homework anymore or not. It was completely effing amazing.

They cried and they cried and, somewhere along the way, somebody had the idea of organizing a Lauren Price Life Celebration, even though she was still very much alive. It was a nice boost for the whole performance, but it was also a major hassle. Lauren's appearances were immediately shortened, as she was forced to race home and delete all the voicemails that people left for mom and dad about donations and stuff.

Without fail, there was always somebody lingering near the pantry, crinkling away just to be rude.

"I see you're still alive," she said.

"I see you're still fat," Lauren said. Isabella crumpled up—her bag, too—and made some dumb sour face. When Lauren turned to leave, she finally decided to get over whatever brat hurdle she was struggling with.

"If you want, I can help you rinse your bandanas out," she said.

"Oh, so you're back on board? What happened, did your boyfriend dump you?"

"No," Isabella said. "And he's not my boyfriend. And it's just that, whatever. Sometimes you gotta put people before yourself, even when they don't deserve it or you don't want to, because that's what it means to be a Price."

A long silence passed as Lauren watched Isabella move back to her snack like she hadn't said anything at all, let alone something so incredibly dumb. Someone sang a dish detergent jingle in the studio and mom and dad clapped and whistled liked they always did with almost everybody.

"You know that's effed up," Lauren said. "You shouldn't do anything for anybody unless they're looking out for you."

"I guess," Isabella said. She folded her snack bag over and over again, all guilty over nothing. "Well in that case, I don't want to help you."

"Fine."

"But I'm looking out for you."

"Whatever."

"I am, you can count on me."

"Fine."

"So, for example, if *this whole thing falls apart*—" Lauren interrupted with a huff. She rolled her eyes so hard something came loose in the back of her head. When she spoke, she did not eff around.

"*Why would the whole thing fall apart?*"

"I'm just saying, if somebody tells or something—"

"Who did you tell?"

"Nobody."

"Who was it? Who? Who? Who? Who? Who?"

"Nobody!" Isabella said. Lauren inched closer and closer across the kitchen. When she got close enough, she slapped Isabella's hands and snatched her wrists up and bent her fingers back. Isabella screamed. She tried to wiggle her way out as her whole body turned red, as she kicked Lauren's shin with the side of her ankle.

"Tell me!" Lauren screamed, "tell me tell me tell me tell me tell me!" Limbs got tangled up in limbs until somebody interrupted with a foot stomp by the toaster. When Lauren looked back, mom and dad and somebody in mime makeup all looked horrified. Lauren released her grip out of sheer disbelief and dad let all of the air out of his body.

"*Who do you think you are?*" he said. Lauren, too, tried to catch her breath and figure it out all at the same time. Isabella wasn't much of a help.

"Lauren told everybody at school that she has cancer and she made me cut my dolls' hair and there's a Life Celebration tomorrow and I have a boyfriend and nobody cares." She got weirdly emotional on that last part, but it was true. Nobody did care. Nobody ever cared about anything either of the Price girls had to say, especially not mom or dad, although that changed rather quickly. Once the mime found his way out, mom and dad told Isabella to go up to her room and think about how many private lessons it would take to replace all of those doll heads, while they made Lauren the center of attention for what felt like the very first time.

"You ought to be ashamed," they said. "That's not who we raised."

"Who *did* you raise?" As soon as it came out of her mouth, Lauren regretted it. Mom got up and headed towards the studio. Near the door, she stopped and lifted her arm, her finger outstretched and shaky.

"Don't you think for a second that I don't own my mistakes." She lingered there for a moment, before finding her light two feet to the left. In one giant step, shifted her body and repeated the same line with greater precision. After that, a true exit.

The door locked behind mom, and Isabella ran down from the steps and tried to knock, but nobody bothered. Dad carried the guilt torch from there.

"I'll tell you what you're going to do," he said. "You're going to go to that celebration and you're going to stand up and tell everybody exactly what you did. And we're all going to sit there and watch you, and you're going to like it."

He was right, in a way. It was everything Lauren dreamt of at one time or another. Undivided attention from everybody, every single set of ears and eyes attached to all the people of Freedom Point that just saw her as her parents' daughter—her parents included. A little piece of Lauren got excited over all of that. Then she realized how awful it would actually be.

When dad went to tend to mom, Lauren snuck upstairs and spent the rest of the night in her room. Crystal&Krystal texted and asked if she wanted to come over and eat ice and look at swimsuits—"assuming u r still alive for summer"—but Lauren passed on the offer. She wondered what Isabella might be up to across the hall, where she went during the whole mess. A hallway light crept in under the door, but when Lauren went to peak outside, it seemed everybody had actually gone to bed. All that remained was a tiny little hush hush violin in the air, from some other bedroom speaker rumble, and when Lauren crept outside, she heard Paolo Sonata singing someone to sleep. Lauren snuck across the hallway carpet and listened closer at Isabella's door and, during the track change, knocked a little bit. The music got even quieter. Lauren knocked again. Somebody sniffled before turning it back up, louder than it was in the beginning. If anybody was listening like Lauren was listening, they'd know exactly what that meant.

THE LIFE CELEBRATION WASN'T ANY EASIER. PEOPLE FILED INTO Freedom Point Junior High through the gym doors, students and townies that got wind of everything. A DJ with a goatee from B77 FM set up under a basketball hoop and started spinning Paolo Sonata's catalogue on shuffle. Everybody got Gatorade, until blue ran out. Nobody wanted any after that. Lauren watched the whole thing from a folding chair up on the stage that somebody's dad built with old risers from Freedom Point Rentals. It was a terrible view. People lingered in and out in awkward hugs and high fives. Two guys helped an old lady with an oxygen tank find a seat near the back row of chairs. Crystal&Krystal pinned Lauren Price memorial buttons on each other, their clothes all awkward and baggy. Lauren watched them struggle and wondered how long it'd be until things got started and she could finally get the whole reveal over with. The set up seemed almost endless and, even when it seemed to slow down, mom and dad and Isabella were still absent. It was a particularly painful death, the cancer. It took forever.

The Freedom Point McDonald's gave out free cone coupons with Lauren's picture on them until Principal McPhee told everybody to find a seat. Students sat with their respective cliques, wedged into the bleachers, under an arch of helium balloons, and everybody else earned metal folding chairs that whined anytime anybody leaned back.

The drama didn't stop there, either. Two women in pantsuits started the whole celebration by talking about their husbands who died from cancer. One of the women handed Lauren an old military portrait.

"He will live on through you," she said, as Lauren felt a heavy block of something in her stomach—hopefully some sort of actual cancer that might have the decency to actually kill her. Crystal&Krystal followed with a karaoke cover of a Michelle Branch song and Miss Cunningham read the lyrics of "I Look To You," but had to start over because Donald Simmons' sign language interpreter couldn't hear her through her sobbing. There was student poetry about how Lauren was like a flower because she was pretty and whatever. Every time the stage cleared, she scanned the audience for her parents, secretly hoping that they were just running late or something. The gym doors would swing open and she'd hold her breath until a man or woman snuck back in with a fussy newborn. It was nice of them to come. Everybody loved little babies, and even they made time to come and support Lauren, and they were only awake for about a minute a day. Grownups and sisters shouldn't have much of a problem, but who really knew. Maybe being a Price didn't mean much of anything anymore.

Somewhere near the end of some tribute, Principal McPhee got all choked up during a slideshow about the big jug of coins that the Sixth Graders saved up for treatment. Then, out of nowhere, he took the time to ask if anyone had ever really been in love before—*really had to provide*, through tick and thin—until somebody peeled him off the stage. The whole thing was so uncomfortable, but not nearly as bad as what was supposed to happen next. Lauren studied the crowd real hard, skipping over anybody that was too tall or too short or dark or light or anything, but, still, nobody had come. When people applauded for what felt like some kind of closing statement prayer, Lauren tried to separate her guilt from her disappointment. She tried to decide what to say or how to say it or why she ought to say it at all anymore. Lauren couldn't think of one person that wanted to hear it or really needed to, either. What was done was effing done, and if anybody learned anything from the whole experience, it wasn't Lauren's right to take it away from them. Nobody should have the power to take anything away like that, not even a Price.

People gathered their purses and backpacks, as Lauren remained seated. The B77 DJ interrupted everybody's exit with an antsy announcement about how some kind of raffle still needed a winner, so it'd be best to listen up. The whole gym got quiet and, without warning, a familiar electric guitar riff sliced right through the whole thing and Lauren's brain and heart instantly imploded. Everybody screamed. Somebody fainted somewhere, and at the end of a long zigzag cord, near the side doors of the Freedom Point Junior High gym, Paolo Sonata appeared.

Bodies dropped all over the place and grown men started sobbing as Paolo headed straight towards Lauren with her face pinned to his shirt. The DJ yelled some kind of unnecessary welcome, but all Lauren could focus on was her heart beat gallop whisper speaker rumble inside her ribs, louder and louder, and the gym got brighter and hotter and Paolo got closer. He looked even less real when he got to the stage and jumped up without using the stairs because that's what it meant to really break the effing rules. Lauren stood up as he waved at all the bystanders and froze as she turned to face her, his whole body covered in white leather and stubble tan and hair gel and eyebrows and sweat. He touched her face on the ribbon on his chest and said something that was probably pure poetry, *real* poetry, but Lauren couldn't hear him because her ears burned so badly, like somebody plugged them back in or something.

Maybe she really did have cancer.

Lauren rubbed her lobes, rubbed the backs of the band-aids until the stickiness started to wear, and Paolo took a mic from the sub nurse whose eyes were red for one reason or another. Paolo moved his hand up and down to tell everybody to settle. When he spoke, he went so slowly. Every word counted. Lauren could vouch.

"Halo. Freedom Point-a. Yunior High."

People cheered because he knew where he was and he pretended like it wasn't the world's biggest disappointment.

"I so hoppy to be here, eh to be with Lo-ran, who is mas beautiful girl." He put his hand on Lauren's back and her ears started burning again. Everything burned at that point. Her blood and her bones. Her vision got sharper, her braids tighter.

People clapped as Paolo took a step towards the audience and took Lauren with him by the hand. All of his magic came through his knuckles and zapped without warning, the whole world wrapped up in his skin on her skin. Paolo waved his hand over the room and Lauren followed with her eyes as he went on with his spell.

"We is here, together," he said, "Because something has to be say about dis town full of all of yous." He took a deep breath and Lauren watched him struggle to find the right words. He could take as long as he wanted for all Lauren cared. There was no way in hell that she was going to announce anything to anybody at that point, not in front of Paolo or his Spanish magic.

"I knows I stands for Lo-ran when I say this things." He stopped for a moment. A single tear formed. A single tear fell. He sucked some snot in. It was the absolute best and it was the absolute worst. Lauren started feel the stomach lump again, for real-for real this time. Paolo went on and squeezed her hand tighter, a rush of blood right through her body. "A-thank you, all to all off you, becuss life iss, iss abou-it dis." Another pause. A balloon popped, somewhere. "Issa abou-it showing up, and this iss what life really a look like." Paolo waved his mic over the gym in slow motion, and Lauren followed and tried to ignore the scenery.

The gym suddenly seemed twice as big, every individual face smaller and smaller, people that Lauren didn't even notice before Paolo started breaking down. People clapped. Lauren swore she heard every individual hand hit every individual hand. Somebody sniffled from 200 feet away and a cell phone buzzed and somebody pulled out a tissue somewhere and blew their nose and let it all out. Paolo gave Lauren a big hug, her chin up on his shoulder and her face to the audience, as she struggled to find something to be proud of.

Paolo parted and went back to his guitar as Lauren stood center stage like some retard with nothing to say. No lines. No artistic choices. No costume changes. No apology. No supervisors. No family. Instead, a sea of her own face staring right back at her. Somewhere in the moment, Paolo started in on some song she'd never heard before.

If anyone was really listening, it sounded like this: Noisy silence sniffle bond. Wet blanket inside shame. Track change, sudden sadness, big mistake on tambourine. Paolo played backup on guitar as Lauren tried to find another lie to get back to whatever seemed like the worst before. Bad luck empty airspace.

Particularly soft bag crinkle.

Careful crowd search.

Longing sort of stomach pit, and, off near the double doors, Isabella with a boy and a poster between them. *You Can Count On Me, Lauren* in big bubble letters. Brand new heartbeat rhythm gallop. Words came up on a pull-down screen and everybody sang together in different voices, Isabella's the loudest.

After some time, a new voice, an onstage interruption. The music slowed and the words froze and Paolo drifted off to the side. The whole production disappeared. Lauren stood at the microphone and asked for everyone's attention for what felt like the very first time.

The Sensational Homer Greeley

IT WAS A UNIVERSAL SHAME THAT THE YEARBOOK BUDGET DIDN'T allow for a scratch and sniff feature. Some might even call it a minor tragedy. The scratch and sniff could've done a whole lot, could've finally untangled everybody from everybody else for a far more vivid rendering of the Eighth Grade class of Freedom Point Junior High. Almost everybody could've been grouped by common scent instead of alphabetical whatever for starters. The jocks—and whatever the wrestlers *really* were—could just be a whole sheet of mildew and deodorant and desperate trophy anxiety. The preps could smell like under polo boob touching and those little bead packets that come with new sneakers, and the vacant squares where their faces ought to be could just be tiny little samples of their girlfriends' body sprays. Vanilla Frosting. Maple Syrup. Moonlit Winnebago Path.

Tally Majors' smell could go on every guy's square.

The weirdos would probably get the last few yearbook pages because there'd be so many different kinds of scents to deal with; daydreamer fog, broken home cigarette boxed dinner, acne picker and thumb sucker sweat. Somebody like Rat Tail might even need his own insert because it'd probably cost a little bit more for the luxury of synthetic dried semen and blood smells, and there'd be almost no other way to keep it from infecting everybody else's personal space—which was, seemingly, Rat Tail's goal, after all. Then again, who knows. Maybe it wouldn't be too far off from Winnebago Moonlit Path.

Some people would be even harder to pinpoint, not because they were so dangerously distinct, but because they didn't have much to them at all. The in-betweeners and the wannabes would have to have their scents updated almost monthly, and, with that, their scents would have to be slightly off every time, like just a little short of anything really credible. They'd probably have to settle for hand soap or something equally inoffensive, sort of a subtle disappearing, maybe a spray or something. That could also benefit somebody like Lauren Price, who moved away after everybody realized she was such a little biotch. The yearbook people would have to be real careful with the disappearing stuff, the spray or whatever it was. Most students wouldn't want to be anywhere near that. That could be another universal shame.

HOMER GREELEY WOULD BE SOME OTHER ISSUE ENTIRELY.

*

NOBODY WOULD BE ABLE TO SCRATCH OR SNIFF HOMER BECAUSE nobody really knew Homer at all. That's who he was, almost fully and completely. Never in a club. Never in a class. Never on a bus route or a phone tree or a roster, but always dressed up, in the middle of a row of yearbook portraits, just in the nick of time. After that, gone, almost completely, until the next one came around.

Though nobody knew Homer, really knew him, everybody knew Homer's mom and all the things she'd drop by the main office for teachers and kids who got bribed to be good. Oatmeal cookies. Chocolate covered blondies. She'd come by and leave some bag of something and drop Homer's backpack off every time he forgot it, and everybody in the office would struggle with who to give it to. Then, at the end of the day, Homer's dad would come pick it back up when Homer forgot to bring it home. That's how it went every day, every week, and then, at the end of the week, for what seemed like centuries, Homer's mom would pop back in to get another copy of the permission slip for the Eighth Grade Earth Science trip to see *Jurassic Park* at the strip mall Cinema 12, because boys will be boys and lose sight of responsibility sometimes. Somebody in the office was always happy to try and help her, even if Cinema 12 closed down five years after Homer died.

Everybody knew that about Homer, the dead part. That's why everybody at Freedom Point had to wear bike helmets, and if they didn't, they got written up and had to help the girls in the office photocopy old Jurassic Park permission slips so that somebody could watch them feel guilty and feel afraid, even more afraid than what was typically allowed for life at ages 12-14. And the helmets had to fit, too, not some eggshell one-size-for-all kind of set up. They had to be custom fit, so that if anybody else's mom forgot to check the rear view mirror in the driveway, they could get hit and still be okay, and get back up and get some kind of shame-fueled second serving of dessert at dinner, and life could just go on without everybody having to make a constant effort all the time.

Nobody ever really said it like that, though. Maybe at one point, but not anymore, Not 20 years after the fact.

On especially bad days, Homer's mom didn't just drop the backpack off. She brought in bowls of soup or cereal, always room temperature, spoon and all, because Homer must've been so busy with his friends that he forgot to eat again. On those days, she'd linger a little longer and then find the courage to ask if she could see the photo they thought they might use for Homer's final school portrait.

"Eighth Grade," she'd say. "This is it."

The girls in the main office kept the photo in an envelope in a drawer with all the spoons Homer's dad didn't have the chance to pick up yet. He never asked to see the photo, so young and so old all at once. Almost filmy, some might say muted, originally printed for the first yearbook, the real one, the one where people definitely remembered Homer for Homer, his scent instead of his legacy, not that that was particularly better. Still, more thorough. More concrete. More honest.

Homer's mom never really said much when the girls in the office brought the photo out. The silence got louder when she got the oxygen tank, when she got older on her own. The picture was just for looking at, until she found the courage to touch Homer's face, and then his hands, and then both of them at the same time. Sometimes she'd pick the photo up and hold it, his whole body in her hands, and smell where his hair hit the light. Then she'd take so much time to put it back down on the desk, as if it were much heavier than she could manage. Nobody in the office answered any phones until she finally found something to say.

"Yes," she'd say, soft and tired. "This is the one." She'd always linger just long enough after that, like she'd realized something or accessed something she had turned off long ago. Homer's dad was to be contacted immediately if anything like that ever happened, but nobody ever needed to call. Homer's mom always found a way to carry on.

"I think he'll like high school. Don't you?" Once everybody in the office agreed, Homer's mom would go back outside and cross the street and head home. She almost always stopped in the driveway, almost waiting for something to appear, before continuing on with whatever needed to be done. The photo would go back in the drawer until somebody else needed it for proof of something.

AT A CERTAIN POINT, IT WAS HARD TO DISTINGUISH WHO WAS REALLY keeping Homer around. For the first little while, when there was just uncomplicated sadness, it was Homer's dad that needed everybody's help and Homer's dad that knew how to ask for it, in memorial trees and candle lightings. People said Homer's mom stayed pretty quiet back then, while Homer's dad figured out how to keep living. That's when they sold the house, the driveway too, and bought a new place near the school so Homer's dad could get a closer view of active energy, of Homer's spirit, before it was time to go back to work.

At some point, Homer's mom seemed to take over the watching. Boys being boys. Girls chasing after them. One little guy outside with no coat, waiting for a ride that forgot the schedule. Rumor had it that Homer's mom tried to snatch him up one time, tried to simply pick him up and carry him away until someone from the office came out and peeled her off as she whispered on about chicken and stars. That's when things got worse and her brain stopped working and nobody, including Homer's dad, had the heart to remind her every morning that whoever she saw in the red sweatshirt wasn't Homer. Neither was the boy popping wheelies or the one with the big poster board in the rain. In a way, it just seemed easier to accept that they were all Homer, that every 14-year-old boy would be Homer, that Homer would magically appear anytime somebody with hair gel and knee scabs and giant backpack went by. At some point, somebody had decided that that's what helped Homer's mom deal with the memory.

Freedom Point never forgot, though, never had the chance or the choice or the heart to. Homer's legacy became their responsibility once Homer's mom started wandering over and asking about the field trip and the photo and the cereal. As long as she stayed, he stayed.

It wasn't all memorial bonsais, though. Boys would be boys, especially the Sixth and the Seventh Graders that weren't old enough to learn the early rhythms of trying to be meaningful, whatever that might look or smell like. When wannabe girls pretended to have nonexistent boyfriends, class clowns would poke fun at Homer's expense.

"Where'd you guys meet, Cinema 12?" they'd say, all amped up on Mountain Dew and invisible testosterone, anytime a glimpse of some picture frame model taped on the inside of a Trapper Keeper.

Someone once spread a rumor that Homer's ghost haunted the girls' locker room, which led to an unfortunate trend in anti-showering.

One Halloween, a bully kid went to Homer's parents' house and asked if Homer was home as a dare for a handful of nougat. Homer's dad called the school the next day. By the time the bully kid graduated, he'd personally copied 492 Jurassic Park permission slips.

Most of the time, however, people were nice, especially the Eighth Graders, the ones that really mattered at the end of the day. Every year, they all got together at the end of the summer with the parents and their teachers talked about the upcoming school year and the perks associated with their imminent departure. Extra spirit days. Peer mentor badges. Vending machine access. The annual class gift, which seemed to always be a flag or a new bench for local stoners to abuse. The assembly would also serve as a small forum for students to propose things they might like the school to give them, as well, which included free reign on chewing gum and cell phones and pocket knives, and, most recently, scratch and sniff yearbooks, which got everybody riled up, which made Principal McPhee shoot the idea down immediately.

"Think about the places your classmates have been," he said, "even just their hands, really, just think about that." People felt weird then. Weirder than usual.

In a triumphant rebound, he said pocketknives could be considered. "But only the kind that don't have corkscrews," he said.

At the end of the night, as with every annual assembly, Coach Henry wrapped the whole thing up with a lecture on being somebody to look up to, which would naturally segue into the deal with Homer's picture and how Homer's mom had been having a hard time lately, which accidentally lasted for 20 years, and it would just be nice if Homer could share the same page with other Eighth Graders as a memorial of sorts, except, if Homer's mother was ever around, it wouldn't be necessary to call it that. Perhaps, it'd be more fitting to choose a club or a team or a class that one might share with Homer if he were still here, if 34 year olds still happened to be in junior high.

The picture always made it in, would probably always make it in. Though Homer's mom could've easily been fooled by the same recycled yearbook each year, and Homer's dad didn't need much of it, either, the endless stream of Freedom Point Junior High Eighth Graders delighted in inviting Homer into their class for a lot of reasons. Sometimes, just because it seemed like the right thing to do, for whoever really loved Homer, wherever they went when he went. Other students said they sort of liked the picture because of tradition, because other kids their same age, who used their same lockers and same textbooks, did it too, and that was enough of a reason to do anything. Most of the time, though, whether anybody actually admitted it to anybody, Homer's picture proved that Eighth Graders do, in fact, happen, and matter, whether they suck their thumbs or eat their feelings or kiss every boy that has a pair of lips, and Freedom Point doesn't forget them, not any of them, not even the ones that don't do nearly enough to have anybody remember much of anything at all. Homer was nobody, or it at least felt that way, and, in that sense, he was everybody, all at once.

MAYBE IT WAS ALL RIGHT THAT THE SCRATCH AND SNIFF STUFF DIDN'T happen. The science behind it needed work and the pages would probably stick and it would be a whole hassle to figure out how to keep all the smells separate. It'd probably be years until someone had the chance or the time or the drive to untangle everybody from everybody else, if it was even an option. By then, Homer's mom would probably be gone in a new way, a more permanent one. Homer's dad, too. By then, it'd be nearly impossible to get the most accurate scent, to *really* locate the essential piece of what it means to be somebody—anybody—especially in a town like Freedom Point.

Acknowledgments

LIKE ANY SMALL TOWN, THIS COLLECTION HAS A REMARKABLE HOME team. When you have a hand, raise a glass:

For New American Press and for David Bowen, who is my favorite David of all the Davids. Thank you for building this wild animal with me. You're better than Bowie.

For Craig Kingston, Angela Welder, Bill Walkner, and all of the high school English teachers who believe in teen writers. I am forever indebted to each of you. Sorry about those two tardies.

For the most incredible CSUN Creative Writing mentors, including Kate Haake, Martin Pousson and Mona Houghton. Thank you for teaching me what the world looks like when you do what you love.

For the Northwestern University MFA dream team, including Stuart Dybek, Steve Amick, Goldie Goldbloom, and Eugene Cross. I will always swoon over your wit, wisdom, and willingness to believe that every draft is something worth talking about.

(Here's where you take an additional shot for Eugene Cross, for being my thesis spirit guide and for always being down to eat tacos and talk about TV. I'd do it all over just to work with you again—except the part where I had to come up with stories when I just wanted to watch TV.)

For all of my friends and fellow writers along the way: I can't thank you enough for helping me, hugging me, and holding my hand through Poetry For Prose Writers. Special shoutout to Gina, Sean, Carrie, Eric, Cara, Kevin, and Ross for writing things that make me want to be better.

For my brothers and sisters, who were the first to teach me how to make useful noise in the world: Greg, Tommy, Amelia, Michael, and Liz—all of whom qualify as super geniuses.

For my parents, Tom and Beth, who, time and time again, teach me to laugh, even when things don't feel so funny. Thank you for believing in every version of me.

Finally, one more sip for A. Brooks Moyer, love of my life, who looks at me like I've written 500 books. With you, words are secondary.

MARINA FRANCES MULARZ holds an MFA in Creative Writing from Northwestern University, where she currently serves as a Fiction Editor for *TriQuarterly Online*. She was the recipient of the 2015 Royal Nonesuch National Humor Writing Prize (sponsored by the Mark Twain House) and a shortlist honoree for *Matrix Magazine*'s LitPOP Award (judged by George Saunders). Most recently, Marina was named a finalist for the Samantha Bee Full Frontal Mentorship Program. She currently lives in Los Angeles and works for Netflix.